W9-AYN-630

It Had Been So Long Since Anyone Had Taken Care Of Her.

So long since she didn't have to think or make decisions. She needed peace, just for a moment. And Sam Beaumont seemed to understand.

Morning birds chirped, their song soothed. Caroline closed her eyes, breathing deeply, fully aware of the man next to her.

He'd been part of the reason she hadn't slept last night. Since her husband had left, Caroline hadn't been held intimately. She hadn't been kissed.

Sam Beaumont had reminded her of all the things she was missing. His kiss, the look in his eyes, right before their mouths touched, was enough to remind her that she wasn't just a single mother raising a daughter alone, but a woman, through and through.

Dear Reader,

When I created the fictional town of Hope Wells, Texas, in my 2005 Silhouette Desire book, *Like Lightning,* the town and the cast of characters I created just wouldn't go away. I fell in love with these people and knew I had to write another Hope Wells story to bring back some of my favorite characters.

Caroline Portman surely has her work cut out for her when mysterious drifter Sam Beaumont enters her life and begins giving her orders at the ranch, as if he's the boss. Belle Star Stables, the ranch Caroline is so desperate to save in this story, was created out of my love for horses. They have always fascinated me and I have always longed for my own horse. And now I have a whole stable…in Hope Wells. I wonder what Caroline would say about that?

Maddie, Trey and Jack Walker, along with my heroine, Caroline, have all returned to tell a heart-tugging story of sacrifice and love and second chances. I hope you enjoy reading Sam and Caroline's story as much as I enjoyed writing it! Also look for my Harlequin Historical novel, *Abducted at the Altar,* coming September 2006, and my Silhouette Desire, *Fortune's Vengeful Groom,* coming in March 2007.

All the best,

Charlene Sands

CHARLENE SANDS

Bunking down with the Boss

Silhouette® Desire

Published by Silhouette Books
America's Publisher of Contemporary Romance

If you purchased this book without a cover you should be aware
that this book is stolen property. It was reported as "unsold and
destroyed" to the publisher, and neither the author nor the
publisher has received any payment for this "stripped book."

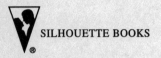

SILHOUETTE BOOKS

ISBN-13: 978-0-373-76746-5
ISBN-10:   0-373-76746-3

BUNKING DOWN WITH THE BOSS

Copyright © 2006 by Charlene Swink

All rights reserved. Except for use in any review, the reproduction
or utilization of this work in whole or in part in any form by any
electronic, mechanical or other means, now known or hereafter
invented, including xerography, photocopying and recording, or in
any information storage or retrieval system, is forbidden without
the written permission of the editorial office, Silhouette Books,
233 Broadway, New York, NY 10279 U.S.A.

All characters in this book have no existence outside the imagination of
the author and have no relation whatsoever to anyone bearing the same
name or names. They are not even distantly inspired by any individual
known or unknown to the author, and all incidents are pure invention.

This edition published by arrangement with Harlequin Books S.A.

® and TM are trademarks of Harlequin Books S.A., used under license.
Trademarks indicated with ® are registered in the United States Patent
and Trademark Office, the Canadian Trade Marks Office and in other
countries.

Visit Silhouette Books at www.eHarlequin.com

Printed in U.S.A.

Books by Charlene Sands

Silhouette Desire

The Heart of a Cowboy #1488
Expecting the Cowboy's Baby #1522
Like Lightning #1668
Heiress Beware #1729
Bunking down with the Boss #1746

Harlequin Historicals

Lily Gets Her Man #554
Chase Wheeler's Woman #610
The Law and Kate Malone #646
Winning Jenna's Heart #662
The Courting of Widow Shaw #710
Renegade Wife #789

CHARLENE SANDS

resides in Southern California with her husband, high school sweetheart and best friend, Don. Proudly, they boast that their children, Jason and Nikki, have earned their college degrees. The "empty nesters" now have two cats that have taken over the house. Charlene's love of the American West, both present and past, stems from storytelling days with her imaginative father sparking a passion for a good story and her desire to write romance. When not writing, she enjoys sunny California days, Pacific beaches and sitting down with a good book.

Charlene invites you to visit her Web site at www.charlenesands.com to enter her contests, stop by for a chat, read her blog and see what's new! E-mail her at charlenesands@hotmail.com.

This book is dedicated to the memory of my childhood friend, Los Angeles County Deputy Sheriff, Jack Miller, the true inspiration for the sheriff in this story. You paid the ultimate price, Jack. Your service and sacrifice will always be remembered.

Special heartfelt thanks to my wonderful editor, Jessica Alvarez. Thank you for all that you do.

One

Tie-One-On Bar and Grill was known for two things: earsplitting country music and beautiful female patrons. Sam Beaumont indulged in both. He sat at a corner table in the honky-tonk listening to Toby Keith's latest, while eyeing a tall blonde up at the bar. She'd caught his attention the minute she walked in. The thing of it was, the Texas bombshell had stared back at him with interest, then spent a minute deep in conversation with the bartender before grabbing two Coors and walking over to him.

"I need a man," she said, with a shake of her head. Her long locks gyrated right back into place. She set the two bottles down on the table and gave him a good long assessing look.

"Yeah?"

"Chuck over at the bar says you might be interested."

He surveyed the leggy blonde, sweeping a leisurely look over her body. She was beauty-queen pretty, but Sam had seen more than a fair share of pretty women in his day. No, it was something in her eyes that spoke to him, a guarded look he knew too well. It was that vulnerability, even as she stood there brazen as all hell, claiming she needed a man, that intrigued him.

Sam sipped his beer slowly, keeping her waiting, and a surge of something he hadn't felt in nearly a year traveled through his veins. An unhurried rush, a tingle of awareness that he had believed long buried, surfaced.

That, in itself, was enough for him to send the woman packing. He didn't *want* to feel anything. Not ever again.

"So are you?" she asked. "Interested?"

He swept her a look. "What'd you have in mind?"

Even through a layer of smoky haze and dim light, he couldn't miss her face color to tomato red, but the woman seemed determined. She slid into the booth at the same time she slid a beer his way. "I need a month's work, for a month's wages, room and board included. Chuck vouched for you. He said you're looking for work."

He sipped his beer and thought about the events that had brought him here. The CEO of a major construction company on the run, not from the law, but from his own guilt-ridden past—Sam was running from things he could no longer face. He didn't need the cash, but hell, staying real busy kept those agonizing thoughts at bay. And Sam needed that, almost as much as he needed his next breath.

"Maybe." He surprised himself with his answer.

Truth be told, he wouldn't mind staying in one place longer than a week. So far, nobody had caught up with him. And he wanted to keep it that way. When he'd left his CEO position with its staggering responsibilities and his old life behind, he'd called his younger brother Wade occasionally, at his insistence, but Sam had never disclosed his location. Trust only went so far. He needed running room and manual labor to keep his tortured mind from remembering.

"I'm Caroline Portman." She held out her hand and Sam took it. Well, hell, he wasn't in the habit of shaking hands with women. But her handshake was firm, even though her skin was soft as butter.

"I'm kinda desperate for help right now, so you can take advantage of me, but only just a little."

She smiled briefly, and he noted two dimples peeking out from both corners of her mouth. Like he said, beauty-queen pretty. He felt another unwelcome surge travel through his body.

"I've got one month to get my place up and running. It's hard work and long hours, but I can pay well."

"What kind of work?"

Sam cursed himself for asking. He'd pretty much determined that those sparks he felt a moment ago weren't anything he wanted to feel again. He'd spent the better part of this year numb to the outside world. Keeping the status quo was essential. If those tiny sparks nudged away the numbness to any degree, then he'd never survive. He'd have to say no to pretty Miss Caroline Portman.

"I'm rebuilding my stables. The place sort of went

downhill, and, well, I'm planning on bringing it back up to the way it was before, uh, before…"

She stopped, blinked several times, biting down on her lip, unable to get the words out. It wasn't an act—he'd had enough experience to know when someone was downright lying. The lady had choked up, and Sam saw the heartache there, the pain she tried so bravely to hold back.

He didn't want to know. He'd had enough grief of his own to last a lifetime. Hell, he'd been drifting for months, heading from one Texas town to another, trying to forget, and that was what kept him going. The forgetting.

He liked this town. Hope Wells reminded him of the place he'd been raised since the age of five, a small friendly place where life was simple and fair. But looking into Caroline Portman's eyes, maybe he needed to amend the fairness part. Sam knew that life held more unfair uncertainties than sometimes a man could take.

Or a woman.

Damn if he didn't love horses. Rebuilding a stable and working with horses again appealed to him. He had spent his young life around ranches. He knew a thing or two about livestock and would enjoy the work, but he still didn't think this a good idea.

"Not interested."

Caroline blinked her big baby-blue eyes.

Sam rose from the table, finishing off his beer. "Thanks for the offer."

Stunned, the blonde sat there wearing a disappointed look.

He set a few bills on the table and strode out of Tie-One-On. If nothing else, meeting Caroline Portman had added a little spice to an ordinary day.

He walked along the sidewalk, heading toward the motel adjacent to the honky-tonk. He'd almost made it to his room, but a shuffling sound from behind alerted him. He spun around.

"Wait up, Mr. Beaumont!"

Caroline Portman walked briskly toward him. Out of breath and flustered, she looked even sexier, like a woman who'd just had a wild night. Sam envisioned putting that look on her face and his momentary slick-hot fantasy made him shudder.

She came up to face him. "I need to know—why?"

"Why?" Sam kept walking, but at a slower pace.

She stayed with him. "Why did you refuse my offer?"

"I don't recall telling you my name," he said, as old instincts kicked in.

"It's a small town. I know a little about you. You're here looking for work, aren't you?"

"Yep."

"I'm offering you a job."

"Yep." He kept walking until he reached his motel room. He leaned against the door to face her. Moonlight streamed onto her form like a spotlight and Sam noticed the snug fit of light-blue jeans and a chambray shirt with some sort of rhinestone work on the chest. Not gaudy, but with style, the color bringing out the true blue in her eyes. She was a woman who didn't flaunt what she had, but yet she couldn't conceal the perfection of her body. "Don't men say no to you very often?"

Caroline blinked and shot him a stern look. "Men say no to me all the time, Mr. Beaumont, but that's not any of your business. I know you're looking for work. The man I had lined up broke his leg, and now I've run out of time. Seems to me we could make some sort of arrangement."

He glanced at his motel door, raising his brows.

"Not that kind of arrangement," she hurried out.

Sam chuckled.

She folded her arms and waited.

Sam pursed his lips. He admired this kind of determination. Damn, if he wasn't the biggest kind of fool. "I need to know something first."

Caroline nodded.

He pulled her into his arms, and leaning back against the door he brought her with him. She was too stunned to protest, so he did what he'd wanted to do the minute he'd laid eyes on her. He kissed her.

It wasn't long, and it wasn't sweet, but rather a deep exploration of lips meeting and mating. Sam steeled himself against her honey-soft mouth. He braced himself against the onslaught of holding a beautiful woman in his arms. He breathed in her female scent, some fruity fresh concoction that reminded him of a lazy summer day, and willed his body not to react. It didn't. Not in the least. Relieved, he released her immediately. He'd learned everything he needed to know.

He stared into furious blue eyes. "I accept the job."

Caroline smiled with sugary sweetness and stepped out of his arms. "Good, because now I can fire you, Mr. Beaumont."

Morning dawned way too fast for a woman who hadn't slept a wink. Caroline Portman rose from bed, dressed quickly and went out to the kitchen to make breakfast. Her head ached and her eyes burned, but she couldn't afford to waste any more time. She had work to do. And keeping busy kept her from thinking about Annabelle, her sweet five-year-old, who she had unselfishly sent off to Florida for a vacation with her grandparents.

How she missed her daughter. She and Annabelle had never been apart. But Caroline's mother and father had insisted on taking Annabelle home with them, especially as they lived just minutes away from every child's fantasy come true, Disney World.

Her parents' offer had come once they'd heard Caroline's plans to refurbish the stables. They had given her their blessing, backing her up one hundred percent. Her parents knew what the stables had meant to her, and how much it had hurt her that her ranch had been run down nearly to ruin. She'd given up her heart and her trust to the man she'd married and he'd abused both. He'd run her livelihood into the ground, putting her so much in debt that she'd only just now surfaced in the black again.

Gil Portman hadn't the mind for business. He'd entered into one bad deal after another, running up bills that he couldn't pay, then trying to recoup the loss by entering into one dubious deal after another. The last one had been investing in a shady stud-service scheme that had nearly bankrupted them. Caroline had been busy raising Annabelle, placing her trust in her husband, but she'd learned a hard lesson with Gil, and she'd never place her life or her livelihood in the hands of another man again. Caroline had vowed when Gil had run off, abandoning his family, that she'd never allow a man to run roughshod over her good intentions again. She knew better now. She could only rely on herself and her two very loving, supportive parents.

Edie and Mike Swenson knew that their daughter would need time alone to achieve her goals without a five-year-old distracting her. They wanted the ranch to succeed again, because they knew that the ranch meant stability for Caroline, but it also meant something more. It meant independence. Caroline needed both now, for herself and for her daughter. Her parents hadn't flinched, but had stepped in, offering to help with her little bundle of energy. And, as they'd put it so tenderly, they'd missed seeing Annabelle. Spending time with their granddaughter would be good for all of them.

Caroline had finally relented, agreeing to let them have Annabelle for one month. In that time, she planned to work harder than she'd ever worked to get her stables back up to par. She'd come up with a new name to signify all the changes she'd planned to make. Annabelle Star Portman would be excited to know that Portman Stables would now be known as Belle Star Stables.

Caroline stuck a piece of sourdough bread in the

toaster oven, set the coffeepot to brewing, then sat down at the table to check the classified ad she'd placed in yesterday's *Hope Wells Reporter*.

The telephone wasn't ringing and no one was breaking down her door looking for work. Her last hope had been dashed yesterday, with Sam Beaumont. But she wouldn't think about him, not when she had a problem to solve. Finding a suitable worker on a temporary basis wasn't easy. But Caroline knew without a doubt she'd have to find someone or her plans for Belle Star would crumble.

Fatigued, Caroline slumped in her seat, struggling to keep her eyes open. She glanced at the *Reporter,* blinking her eyes, but the newspaper print blurred, her eyelids drooped and her mind all but shut down. Maybe if she just slept for a few minutes, she'd feel better.

Maybe if she laid her head down on the table, just for five minutes…

The explosion rocked Caroline to a sitting position. She snapped her head up from the kitchen table where just minutes ago, she'd laid her head down to rest. Dazed from her little nap, it took a moment for her to come to grips with what just happened. Her toaster oven had overheated. The appliance, literally "toast" now, had ignited the can of cooking spray she'd left nearby. Caroline was covered with the greasy effects of that combustion.

And within seconds, flames erupted, catching on to the overhead oak cabinets.

Caroline screamed, "Oh God!"

She ran for the fire extinguisher on the wall next to the refrigerator and yanked it free. Fumbling with the handle, she couldn't get it to work. She'd never used an extinguisher before. Heat burned her cheeks and smoke billowed from the cabinets. The fire spread.

Panicked, she fidgeted again with the extinguisher and cursed the husband who'd left her in this mess, the husband who'd abandoned his wife and child when the going got rough, the husband who had recently died, leaving her a widow. "Damn you, Gil!"

She didn't take time to worry about speaking ill of the dead. Since Gil had abandoned his family, nothing much had gone right in her life. She couldn't help but lay the blame where it seemed to fit. Marrying Gil had been the biggest mistake she'd ever made, yet without him, she wouldn't have had Annabelle. That was the only good thing he'd ever given her.

Caroline gave up on the extinguisher, opting to call the fire department instead. Of course, she knew her entire kitchen might burn to the ground before they arrived, but she had little choice.

And then the choice was taken from her.

A pair of masculine hands reached out to grab the extinguisher. Stunned, Caroline turned sharply to find *him*, the man who had caused her sleepless night, standing beside her, taking control.

"Get back," Sam Beaumont said, commanding her with a quick nod.

Caroline stepped back and watched as he pulled the pin and operated the fire extinguisher, putting out the flames with long sweeping motions. He did a thorough job, making sure all the flames were put out, before turning to look at her. "You okay?"

Numb, she nodded, biting her lip.

He swept a quick gaze over her body as if he had to make sure himself. She must have passed inspection because he set the extinguisher down and assessed the damage to her cabinets.

Caroline glanced at her once-tidy kitchen, where just minutes ago everything had been neat and organized. Now, the place looked like a disaster, but her kitchen was still standing, and so was she. "What are you doing here?"

He turned to face her, his lips quirking up in a charming smile. "Apparently, putting out your fire."

Tears stung her eyes, from the smoke and the flames and from the relief she felt at this moment. She gazed into Sam Beaumont's dark-brown eyes, seeing not the hard man who had refused her yesterday, but a man who appeared genuinely concerned. He'd shown up in the nick of time.

And Caroline owed him. But he still hadn't explained what he was doing here.

"Want to tell me what happened?"

Caroline shrugged, numbed from the thought of what might have happened. The little appliance mishap might have escalated into a full-blown house fire if Sam Beaumont hadn't shown up. "I guess the toaster oven overheated. It's old and I should have known the other day when…it…sparked…that I…" A lump formed in Caroline's throat. She couldn't finish her thought.

Sam took her arm gently and guided her out of the kitchen. "Let's get away from this smoke."

He opened the back door and they both stepped outside. The fresh air was like a balm to her out-of-whack nerves. She breathed in deeply.

"Wanna sit?" he asked and led her over to the back-porch swing. She sat down, and to her surprise he took a seat right next to her.

Still reeling in shock, Caroline remained quiet. It had been so long since anyone had taken care of her. So long since she didn't have to think or make decisions. She needed peace, just for a moment.

And Sam Beaumont seemed to understand. He sat beside her in silence.

Morning birds chirped, their song a harmonious cluster of sounds that soothed. Caroline closed her eyes, breathing deeply, listening, fully aware of the man next to her.

He'd been a major part of the reason she hadn't slept last night. Since her husband had left nearly two years ago, Caroline hadn't had any physical contact with a man. She hadn't been held intimately. She hadn't been kissed.

Sam Beaumont had reminded her of all the things she was missing. He'd taken her into his arms, pulled her close and brought his mouth to hers. He'd made her feel feminine and alive with just one kiss. He'd sparked something in her that Caroline had buried a long time ago. She knew she was no longer that young, naive, innocent girl who believed in happily ever after. No, a bad marriage had erased all of those thoughts, but she hadn't realized that she'd been dry, like an arid desert, wasting her womanhood away.

Sam Beaumont's kiss, the look in his eyes, right before their mouths touched, was enough to remind her that she wasn't just a single mother raising a daughter alone, but a woman, through and through.

Enough of a woman to realize that the man sitting next to her was sexy as sin. The tight fit of his jeans and the broad expanse of his shoulders hadn't escaped her.

"It's nice out here," he said.

Caroline nodded in full agreement, but then she turned to look at him as curiosity set in. She asked once again, "What are you doing here?"

He didn't hesitate this time. "I could lie and say I was passing by on my way out of town. That's what I'd planned on saying. But the truth is, I found your ad in the newspaper and came out here deliberately."

"Why?" Caroline asked, realizing she should be concentrating on how to fix her newly burned kitchen cabinets instead of shooting the breeze with Sam Beaumont, but somehow she couldn't quite tear herself away. She had questions for him and she hoped he would give her the satisfaction of truthful answers.

"I came here to apologize."

"Oh." It was the last thing she expected him to say. Caroline wasn't accustomed to having men apologize to her. Gil hadn't had the civility or manners to do so.

His arrogance wouldn't allow it. Caroline only saw her husband's good side when he wanted something from her. And sadly, she hadn't realized his tactics until after he'd abandoned his family. She'd been blinded by love, or what she'd thought was love, and now, as she gazed into Sam Beaumont's dark eyes, she wondered if she could believe him.

"I stood behind your door, ready to knock, when I heard the explosion. Then I heard you scream. Your door was open, and, by the way, you should keep your doors locked, especially when you're all alone out here. The rest is history."

Caroline stared out into the morning light, squinting her eyes and holding her breath. "You say you came to apologize?"

"I was way out of line yesterday. It kept me from sleep last night and I knew I had to make it right."

So, she hadn't been the only one who hadn't had a good night's sleep. She felt herself softening to him. It seemed he had scruples and a conscience, but she wasn't letting him off so easily. She'd learned her lessons the hard way. "I see. So was it your refusal, the kiss or your arrogance that you're apologizing for?"

Sam chuckled and lifted up from the swing to lean against the porch post. He faced her squarely. "I deserved that."

"I know," she said, but a smile she couldn't contain emerged. There was something extremely charming about the man, yet, Caroline wouldn't let her guard down completely. She stood up to face him. "What I can't figure is why you kissed me."

Sam's gaze traveled to her chest as sunlight beamed down. She felt piercing rays of heat, not from the sun but from his direct perusal.

He ran a hand down his face and finally, he lifted his eyes to hers. "You've got, uh, something wet splattered on your blouse."

Caroline glanced down. She'd been through too much this morning to be embarrassed, but the fact remained that she'd been splattered with cooking spray, and grease stains made her blouse almost transparent. And of course, the moisture had hit the most protruding target. Her breasts. She folded her arms over the wet area, hiding what he'd already seen. "Hazards of wet cotton."

Sam agreed, "Yeah, what a bummer."

She caught his smile, but he had the good grace to maintain eye contact with her.

"Will you answer my question?"

He set both hands in the back pockets of his jeans and sighed quietly. "Why does a man kiss a beautiful woman?"

Caroline soaked up the compliment. Oh God, did it feel good to hear those words. Yet she steeled her resolve, not letting him off the hook so easily. She had to know. "You tell me."

Sam averted his gaze, looking off in the distance. She doubted he was studying the scenery. After all, broken-down barns and stables, along with a neglected yard chock-full of weeds, weren't all that interesting.

"Okay," he said, "you deserve the truth. It was a test."

"And I passed? Or failed?" Caroline tried to make sense from his words.

He shook his head. "Don't take this the wrong way, but the test had nothing to do with you. It was *my* test. I had to know something."

"What? What did you have to know? I offered you a job and you kissed me? What kind of test was that?" Caroline asked, exasperated. She didn't understand any of this. The man seemed to be speaking in riddles.

Sam just stood there, looking guilty.

It was that look that got her to thinking. Then, as if a light clicked on in her head, she figured it out. "You kissed me to see if you were attracted to me," she stated with certainty. "And…and once you did…you accepted the job."

Sam's mouth twisted.

"Meaning, you decided you could work with me…because…because…" Caroline blinked her eyes, keeping both fury and tears in check as the niggling truth began to surge forth in her mind.

"Look, it was a mistake, a damn fool thing to do. But you've got one heck of an ad campaign, lady, walking up to me in that bar claiming you're looking for a *man*. I'm just looking for work. Period."

"I could have phrased that better," she said defensively, "but you had no right to put me to your test."

Caroline closed her eyes, willing away the pain as realization dawned quite clearly. Sam Beaumont had made her come alive last night, with a hungry mouth and steady embrace. He'd made her feel things she hadn't felt in years, while she, on the other hand, had been so uninspiring that he'd decided he could work with her. She wouldn't be a temptation at all. Caroline Portman wouldn't shake his resolve in any way.

Caroline didn't think her day could have gotten any worse. Sam Beaumont had touched her last night with an embrace and sexy kiss that had revived what she believed dead inside in one quick unexpected moment.

"Look, I'm here to apologize. I know I made a mistake. And I'm real sorry."

Caroline heard the sincerity in his tone. She stared deeply into his eyes and saw it there, too. His expression never faltered, the apology written all over his handsome face. For some strange reason, she believed him. Which was saying something. After what Gil had put her through, Caroline didn't put much faith in any man. "Okay, I accept your apology."

"Listen, let me put my words into action. Since I'm here anyway, and I know a thing or two about carpentry, I can fix your cabinets for you. Unless you've hired someone already?"

She shook her head.

"It'll take me the rest of the day, but I'm not heading anywhere special, so I don't mind doing the work."

Caroline inhaled deeply. The offer had merit. "I don't know if I can afford you."

"No charge," he said immediately.

"That's not what I meant, Sam."

He stared into her eyes for a long moment. Too bad he had a sinful body, a handsome face and dark eyes that could burn into your soul, because sexy Sam Beaumont found Caroline completely lacking as a female. Boy, she didn't know if she'd ever get over that one.

"I'll be on my best behavior."

She could bank on that but the thought didn't comfort her. Sam wasn't good for her ego, but Caroline had put that part of her life on hold anyway, so what did it matter if she wasn't the kind of woman Sam Beaumont thought attractive? Right now, all she needed to know was if he could help her out with her cabinets. "You sure you know how to fix cabinets?"

"I've had some experience." He peered at the damage with a gleam in his eyes as if calculating exactly what he needed to do and how he'd accomplish it.

It was good enough for Caroline. She surely didn't know anything about repairing them and it didn't look as if anyone else was coming to her rescue today. "You're on."

He nodded, then approached her with a purposeful stride. Their gazes locked as he stood before her. "Tell me something."

His probing look told her she wasn't going to like his question. "What do you want to know?"

"When I was behind your door, I heard you scream out. So, who's Gil?"

Two

Caroline appeared shaken by his question. She'd flinched when he'd mentioned Gil's name, and then a somber expression stole over her face. For a moment, Sam thought she'd keep that information to herself, but then she spoke up, albeit quietly. "Gil was my husband. He died about four months ago."

"Sorry. That's rough." How well he knew about losing someone you loved. How well he knew the heartache involved, the day-to-day agony of living without the ones you love. Sam hadn't been able to face his demons any longer. He'd taken off trying to escape the truth, to dull the pain, to find some way of surviving.

Caroline sighed, a brief smile emerging before she spoke. "As long as we're being honest with each other, I can tell you that Gil only did two really good things in his life. He gave me a daughter for one. She's five years old and the light of my life. And two, he kept up his life insurance. We have enough money to live and, if I'm real careful, there'll be enough to refurbish our ranch."

Caroline had a five-year-old daughter? Sam's gut clenched. A searing jolt shot straight through him and he winced as if he'd been sucker-punched. He hadn't suspected, though he should have known she might have been married, she might have had a family.

"Where is your daughter?"

"Annabelle?" A winsome expression stole over her face and she smiled. Sam saw the joy there and the love she wouldn't even try to hide. God, if only Sam had shown that same kind of love to his own daughter. If only he'd been…more. "She's with her grandparents in Florida. They've got her for the whole month. I miss her terribly."

Sam missed his daughter, too. Only she wasn't ever coming home. His heart ached and old pain surfaced. Pain he'd tried to run from. He'd endured months and months of agonizing grief and then it had turned to numbness. He liked the deadened feeling best. He'd managed to drift for months this way. Forgetting.

Good God, Caroline's daughter was the same age his daughter would have been—had she lived.

And little Tess *would* have lived if Sam had been there for her.

"My parents took her so that I could have this month to bring Belle Star Stables up to snuff again."

Sam brought himself back to the present. "So, you need to find help really fast."

She nodded. "Time's a wasting."

"Any prospects?"

"None at all."

Sam pondered this for a moment. His first instincts were to get out of Dodge the minute Caroline confessed to having a young daughter. Sam didn't think he could take the day-to-day reminder, but her daughter wasn't here. And she wouldn't be for a month.

And Sam had had enough of drifting from town to town every few days. He wouldn't mind staying on in Hope Wells for the month. But he'd already made a big mistake with Caroline and he'd hurt her feelings, as well.

He figured he'd be doing her a favor if he stayed on. He knew his way around a ranch and truth be told he'd spent the better part of his adult life running one of the largest construction companies in the southwest, the Triple B, his father's namesake, Blake Beaumont Building. He'd been CEO and top of his game, professionally. He'd helped his father bring in more business than they could handle, building up a small enterprise into a multi-million dollar corporation. To say he had some experience in carpentry was an understatement. Sam had made a fortune, but he'd paid a heavy price for his success. The cost of his dedication to work had been the untimely death of his child.

Yet as he stood there, looking at Caroline, he knew he could help her. If she'd agree, he could have her place up and running in one month's time, then he'd move on. Actually, he missed the hands-on work of creating and building something from scratch. Refurbishing her stables would be a challenge he'd love to take head-on.

And he'd already determined he could work side by side with Caroline, pretty as she was, he simply wasn't interested in getting involved with a woman. Good thing too, because the whole widow-and-child package would do him in otherwise.

"Listen, I have a proposition for you. If by the end of the day, you like the work I've done, and if no one comes knocking on your door for the job, I'm reapplying."

Caroline lifted her brows. "You are?"

"Yep, if you're agreeing."

She folded her arms, contemplating. "I don't see as I have much choice."

"Fair enough. Is it a deal then?"

Caroline hesitated, but he knew he had her over a barrel. She was desperate for help. One determined lady. She had a plan in mind, and Sam had no doubt she would succeed, with his assistance. "Let's see what you can do with those burned-up cabinets."

"Yes, ma'am."

Caroline reassessed the damage, not to her kitchen, but to her heart, and decided that it was a good thing Sam Beaumont was only interested in an honest day's work. He'd been up front about it. He'd been truthful. That's a heck of a lot more than she'd ever gotten from Gil.

Caroline had more than her ego on the line. And if

Sam Beaumont was the man for the job, then she was one step closer to seeing her dream come true. She hadn't gone into that honky-tonk last night looking for love. She'd gone looking for an employee.

Caroline grabbed the bag of food she'd bought from Patsy's Pantry, burgers fully loaded, fries and two caramel and fudge sundaes, still frozen she hoped, and exited her truck. She'd left the house three hours ago to run errands and then, because her kitchen was in turmoil, she'd picked up dinner.

It was after seven o'clock when she walked through her front door. Sam had been working all day, and if the cabinets looked half as good as the man fully immersed in the job, wearing a tight white tank and those faded blue jeans, then Caroline had found herself an employee.

"Dinner," she announced, setting the bags on the kitchen table.

When she glanced up, she found Sam standing back from the cabinets, admiring his work. "Almost through," he said.

Caroline swallowed, looking at the work he'd done. He'd managed to reface the existing cabinets so that they appeared an identical match. No one would have guessed that there had been burnt and charred wood there just hours ago. "They're beautiful."

"I couldn't find a match to the old doors, so I put on all new ones."

"I see that." Caroline loved the new look, but she hesitated. "I hadn't planned on renovating my entire kitchen. Those new doors must have been expensive."

"Nah," Sam said, finally glancing over to her. His dark eyes twinkled and Caroline's stomach flip-flopped. He was a man who, when he gave a woman his full attention, could turn her inside out. "I made the lumber store manager a deal. Trust me, you got more than a fair shake on the doors."

"How?"

"How'd I make the deal?" He seemed pleased with himself. "You'll do all your lumber business with him during the renovations and you'll give his kid free riding lessons."

"Free riding lessons?"

"Yep, you were planning on giving lessons, weren't you?"

She chuckled. "I am now."

Actually, aside from boarding and grooming the horses, Caroline had toyed with the idea of giving lessons after school and on weekends. Sam had just cemented the notion into reality.

He set the invoice for the cost of the lumber, doors included, onto the kitchen counter. Caroline leaned over to take a look. She couldn't fault him for being excessive since he had indeed gotten a fair price for the materials. She glanced up to meet his eyes. "Looks like I can afford you after all."

"So I'm hired?"

Caroline nodded. "For the month. Yes, I'll hire you. And I don't plan on starving my one and only employee. I brought dinner home from Patsy's Pantry. It's nothing fancy but the food's the best in five counties. Hungry?"

"I could eat," Sam admitted, "but I'd like to clean up first. Mind if I take a shower?"

A shower? Caroline's mind spun in a dozen directions, but it came back to earth quickly and focused on one final thought. Sam Beaumont, with his bronzed skin and strong body, *naked*, in her shower. The instant mind flash caused her a moment of doubt in hiring him.

He was good-looking to a fault. And sexy as sin.

Oh, Caroline, get a life.

"Sure, you can take a shower. Follow me."

Caroline grabbed a towel from the linen closet on her way toward the bathroom. "Sorry, all I have is this color."

Sam took the fluffy flamingo-pink towel. "Thanks. As long as it dries my bones, I'm happy."

"Take your time," she said once they reached the bathroom. "Dinner will keep." With that, Caroline headed for the kitchen, blocking out the image of hot steamy water running down Sam's bare body. Instead, she was grateful that Sam didn't have one of those macho, don't-give-me-anything-pink attitudes so many men share. A real man is secure enough in his own skin not to worry about trivial things like that. A real man knows who he is, and what he's made of.

It had taken Caroline twenty-nine years to realize what made a real man, and unfortunately, she just hadn't met too many of that breed in her lifetime.

She entered the kitchen, setting out paper plates and napkins, two glasses of lemonade and then... She remembered the fudge and caramel sundaes! "Oh, no!"

Quickly, she dug into the bag and came up with both ice cream concoctions. She sighed with relief. They weren't completely melted, so she set them into the freezer, hoping for the best.

Not ten minutes later, Sam reentered the kitchen. He'd dressed in his jeans again, but his chest was bare. Caroline blinked, opened her mouth to speak, but no words came out. Her naked-shower fantasy didn't compare to seeing the real thing. His jeans hung low, dipping under his navel and hugging a tight butt in the back. His chest, wasn't massive, wasn't muscle-man broad. No, it was simply the perfect amount of bronzed strength.

With hair slicked back, and tiny beads of moisture still caressing his skin, he headed straight for her in a slow sexy saunter. Sharp tingles coursed through her body as he came closer. Caroline held her breath, unable to move, staring.

"Excuse me," he said, passing her to reach for his shirt hanging on the back of the kitchen chair, the one he'd removed just before he began ripping out the damaged cabinets. He slipped his arms into the sleeves and turned to face her, buttoning up. "Smells good."

Her shoulders slumped ever so slightly "Oh, uh, yes. Let's eat."

Fantasy over.

And it was a good thing, too. Because if Sam Beaumont had reached for her hand, Caroline would have followed him.

Right into the bedroom.

* * *

"I'd like to seal the cabinets tonight, so I can get started tomorrow with the stables. The doors I can do outside, but I'm going to have to put the sealant on the existing cabinets where they are. Only problem is that the fumes will be too strong for you to sleep in the house."

Sam Beaumont collected his paper trash, helping Caroline clean up the kitchen after they'd eaten their meal. She wiped down the counter and table then turned to him. "Not a problem really. I can sleep in one of the stable stalls tonight."

"Are you sure?"

She shrugged. "The cabinets need to be finished. And I've got a sleeping bag. I've slept out there before."

"Oh, yeah? Have you lived here all of your life?"

"Most. When I married Gil, my parents retired and moved to Florida. They gave us the stables to run as a wedding present, along with the house I'd grown up in. They weren't crazy about changing the name of the stables to Portman, but they'd agreed. Gil had a thing about that. Status was everything to him. I should have known better, but I agreed, too. After all, I'd married into that name. At least when the place went to the dogs, my parents' name wasn't associated with the stables any longer. They'd worked hard most of their life to build up what Gil ruined in just four short years."

Caroline didn't want sympathy. And Lord knows, she'd agonized about this for too long. She wasn't looking back any longer. She had a future now, with the life insurance money that she'd received. And she was determined to create a good life for Annabelle in the process. One day, her daughter would have everything.

"Well, sounds like we've got a lot of work ahead of us. It'll take me an hour or two to get these cabinets sealed. And I can guarantee that you won't want to be in here."

Us? Caroline hadn't been one half of "us" in a long time. She'd been the one making all the decisions, doing all the planning and *hoping.* She sorta liked the sound of it, even as she reminded herself that the sexy drifter she'd hired would only be here for one month.

Caroline knew she to had take complete control—relinquishing her part in the ranch had been a mistake she would never make again. She had too much to lose now. She'd barely squeaked by these past few years, boarding a few horses and taking on odd jobs just to earn enough to keep food on the table and the bankers from knocking on her doors. She'd never risk her daughter's future again. And she'd never lay her heart and her life on the line for another man. So this one-month arrangement with Sam Beaumont was a perfect solution.

"Okay, well, I'll just muck out some of the stables. I've got to check on Dumpling, anyway. She misses me if I don't spend time with her at night."

"Dumpling?"

"Our family mare. She's a sweetheart."

He nodded. "So, will I be sleeping in the stables too?"

Caroline's mind once again flashed a thrilling image of Sam Beaumont waiting for her on a plush bed of hay. Her heart danced for a moment and, inwardly, she sighed. "No, there's a room at the back of one of the stables. Used to be a tack room, but I recently converted it into a guest room. I wouldn't expect much, but there's a comfortable bed, a dresser and electricity."

"Sounds fine."

But Sam Beaumont had already dismissed Caroline, focusing his attention on the cabinets. He worked his hands over the wood, looking for rough spots, surveying the job ahead.

Chuck from the Tie-One-On had been right in vouching for Sam Beaumont. He seemed intent on getting the job done and oddly enough, despite the way they'd met, Caroline felt she just might be able to work with him.

She reminded herself to ask Chuck how he'd come to know so much about Sam, and why he seemed so eager for her to hire him.

Sam Beaumont still was a mystery to her, the handsome drifter who seemed far too capable a man to be scrounging around for work, traveling from town to town like a vagabond.

The smell of wood and hay, of horse dung and leather brought back memories of happier times in Sam's youth. Sam stepped into the room he'd be staying in, breathing deeply, glancing around the small twelve-by-twelve room. He'd frequented the best five-star hotels in the country, but this room with its blue-checkered curtains, rough wood-framed landscapes and mismatched furniture, appealed to him in ways those elegant suites never had.

He and his younger brother, Wade, had been shoved

off to live with their Uncle Lee and Aunt Dottie on their working cattle ranch near El Paso. They'd had a small herd, earned a decent living and Sam would like to think he and Wade had brought some joy into their lives. His aunt and uncle couldn't have children of their own, and Sam's father thought it fitting to get the boys out of his hair while he built his new company from the ground up. Uncle Lee and Aunt Dottie had been the only true parents he and Wade had ever known.

Sam set his duffel bag on the bed then plopped down to test the mattress. Comfortable, he assessed, lying down and stretching out his legs. He laced his hands behind his head and rested on a navy corduroy pillow. He stared up at the ceiling, looking for a kind of peace that always seemed to elude him.

Sam had seen action in the Persian Gulf War, he'd battled the toughest opponents in the business world, but he had never known the kind of fear he experienced each night when he closed his eyes.

Thoughts of Tess would surface. But his mind denied Sam the sweet memories of his daughter. He didn't deserve them, not yet. Not ever. Sam had lost so much that day, his daughter, a wife who had blamed him, and the better part of his soul. "I'm sorry, Tess," he whispered quietly. "So sorry, sweetheart."

Sam rose from the mattress and paced the floor. He had no intention of sleeping on this comfortable bed tonight. He grabbed the doorknob and yanked open the door.

Caroline Portman stood on the other end, balancing a tray, ready to knock.

"Uh, hi," she said, "I almost forgot about dessert." She lifted the tray to his eyes. "Ice cream sundaes, slightly melted, but delicious all the same." She walked past him, stepping into the room. "Are you settled in for the night?"

"Not really. I won't sleep here tonight," he announced, "while you're sleeping on a bale of hay."

She grinned and those twin dimples peeked out. "I don't mind."

"I do. You get this bed tonight, or the deal's off."

"Really?"

"Yeah, really. The lady always gets the bed."

Caroline tilted her head to one side and smiled. "That's really not necessary."

Sam stared, standing still in silent argument, his expression set in stone.

Caroline sent him a look of genuine appreciation. "Okay, and thank you. That's very…very sweet." Sam got the distinct feeling she hadn't been treated with regard too often.

He wouldn't belabor the point. Instead, he glanced at the sundaes. "Those look good."

"Let's sit outside and eat them," she said, "before they melt even more."

They opted for a bale of hay just outside the barn. The night was warm, the sky overhead twinkling with bright stars. Sam enjoyed the serenity. He took a deep breath, and Caroline's fresh fruity scent invaded his brief peace. He glanced at her as she ate with gusto, devouring her ice cream. Sam found little enjoyment in life, but watching someone eat with such obvious glee made him smile.

"What's funny?" she asked, catching him.

Sam shook his head and pointed to her empty dish. "You ate that like there's no tomorrow."

His observation didn't rattle her; she grinned. "I know. I don't indulge often, but when I do, *watch out*."

Good Lord, she looked pretty, sitting under the stars with moonlight streaming down. She had the softest features, a sweet smile and beautiful blue eyes. And Sam wondered about her comment. What other things did she indulge in? Her "watch out" statement intrigued the hell out of him. No, he wouldn't allow his mind to go there.

"You saved the day, Sam. I want to thank you for coming to my rescue today." Again, the sincerity in her tone made him think this woman, who deserved more, hadn't been treated with much regard in the past.

"I'm far from a hero, Caroline."

Caroline set the empty plastic ice cream dish on her lap and with head downcast, she admitted, "Still, I'm glad you're here."

"Because the stables mean everything to you."

She nodded. "My heart's been broken, Sam. I can't ever let that happen again."

Sam knew how she felt. Her sentiments echoed his own. Losses of any kind were hard to take—there was no way to measure the amount of pain they caused. Sam didn't think he had an exclusive on heartache. Obviously, Caroline had had a bad marriage and had almost lost her precious ranch. "We've got a lot of work to do starting tomorrow. Let's get some sleep."

Caroline agreed. She stood up abruptly, dropping the

dish and napkin that had been on her lap. Both went down to retrieve the items. They reached for the dish at the same time and bumped heads.

Sam's hand covered hers and an electric shock traveled through his system. Her sweet laughter rang out, tempting his senses. His body instantly reacted. Not just a little slight jab, but a full-fledged, piercing arrow that angled straight to his groin.

He went thick and hard below the waist. He summoned all his willpower to contain his massive erection. Wasn't happening. Instead, white-hot desire bulleted through his body. He ached from the fullness, something he hadn't experienced in a long time. That dead part of his body came alive and no matter how hard he tried to bring the numbness back, he couldn't.

Sam released Caroline's hand and backed off, staring into her eyes. Had he lied to himself last night when he'd kissed her? Had he persuaded himself that he was immune to her soft lips and warm womanly body? Had he fooled himself into thinking that Caroline Portman hadn't intrigued him from the very start, approaching him with her I-need-a-man, comment?

Sam didn't have answers. What he had was a hard-on that was killing him.

"Sam?" Caroline looked at him with curious eyes.

"It's nothing, Caroline. I'll see you in the morning." Stiffly, Sam rose and headed for the stable stall where he'd be sleeping tonight.

And he was hoping that when he woke, this momentary lapse would disappear in the morning's light.

Three

"**Y**ou are a beauty," Sam admitted, stroking her female body, closing his eyes for a moment, relishing the feel of such a lovely creature. It gladdened his heart to see that she responded in kind.

"I see you've met Dumpling," Caroline said, walking up to the mare's stall. "And it appears you've made a new friend."

Sam patted the mare with affection. "She's a sweetheart, just like you said."

Caroline approached, rubbing her cheek against the mare's snout. The animal responded with a soft whinny. "Yeah, Dumpling and I go back a long way."

She eyed the horse with tenderness; her face glowing and Sam figured she saved that look for only those who'd earned it—only those she trusted.

"How'd you sleep?" she asked. When she turned her attention and her baby blues on him, Sam inwardly flinched, the blow taking him by surprise. Those sparks, those damned unwelcome fireworks hadn't disappeared as he'd hoped. They were alive and well and residing uninvited and unwelcome, flaming up his body. At least his anatomy below the waist hadn't betrayed him. Yet.

"Fine."

She narrowed her eyes. "Really? Were you comfortable in the sleeping bag?"

Last night Sam had had visions of lying with Caroline in the sleeping bag, counting stars and making love. He'd willed the sensation away, but the powerful urge only grew stronger. Unable to fight it off, he'd wanted to get up and run for the hills, but Sam had had enough of letting people down in his life. This time, he would keep his promise to work here for the month. He'd given his word, and he wouldn't back out now.

Caroline believed he wasn't interested in anything but an honest day's work and that's how he would keep it, as difficult as that would be.

"I slept just fine."

"Me, too." She sighed breathlessly. "Best sleep I've had in a long while, even though I miss Annabelle something fierce."

Sam turned away at the mention of the little girl's name. He had yet to come to terms with the death of his daughter. He didn't begrudge Caroline's love for her little girl, but the ache inside him burned deep and tore at him with raw agonizing pain. He couldn't hear talk of her little Annabelle without reliving the horrible day that young Tess had died.

Sam blamed himself.

And he always would.

He peered out over the yard and the other buildings they'd be working on and quickly changed the subject. "Do you have a plan of action?"

Caroline sidled up next to him. "After breakfast, I was hoping we could go over what needs doing. We could make a list of repairs. As you can see, the yard itself is pretty run down."

Sam glanced her way, seeing so much in her eyes, her hopes and expectations and her dream of a successful stable coming alive again. "I think that's a good plan. But I'm not one for breakfast."

She smiled. "Coffee then?"

"Sounds good."

"Well then, I'll go get it brewing and bring you out a cup. Sound fair?"

"You're the boss."

She lifted her lips in a soft smile. "I am, aren't I?"

Her scent lingered as he watched her walk into the house, her perfect derriere catching his eye. She moved with grace, the unintentional sway of her hips purely natural. She wore a plaid work shirt and ripped jeans. Work clothes. Yet Sam eyed her with more enthusiasm than he would an exotic dancer working a dance pole.

His body reacted, tightening up.

He cursed and grabbed a steel rake. He'd just burn off

his extra energy with good hard work. He wasn't above mucking out a stall, and from what he could tell there would be plenty of stalls to muck in the very near future.

Later that day, Caroline cooked spaghetti and meatballs and they ate dinner together in the kitchen, each absorbed in their own thoughts, or so it seemed. The radio, set on low, played down-home country tunes, easing the quiet. All in all, Caroline was pleased with the day's work they'd put in. Sam had proven himself a hard worker and a man of his word. So far.

But Sam didn't divulge too much about himself. And Caroline wasn't into prying. She knew what she needed to know about Sam Beaumont for now.

"So do you think we can finish everything on our list before the month is up?" Caroline asked, stringing a wad of spaghetti around her fork. She'd posed this question to Sam in different ways today and each time his reassurance had helped calm her nerves.

"I think so. There're major repairs to be done to the roofs and stable stalls, some painting and shoring up of your fences. The yard will need a complete overhaul. You'll need new supplies of feed and hay. But I think we can do it."

Caroline nodded. "Yes, I'm hoping so. I'd like to have everything done before school starts. Annabelle will be starting first grade. She'll be gone most of the day. I'll be able to run things, along with some part-time help."

"Do you have anyone in mind?"

She shrugged, not worried in the least. "There's

always high-school students ready to earn some extra cash. I know because I used to be one of them." She chuckled, recalling her days as a part-time employee. "I worked at Curly's Ice Cream Parlor, making root beer floats and banana splits after school."

Even though they spoke of nothing specific, Caroline enjoyed conversing with another grown-up. And this particular grown-up happened to make her heart stop every now and then when she least expected it. Sam Beaumont had a style all his own. His quiet demeanor, his work ethic and his incredible good looks blended into a man who had, to put it quite simply, entered into Caroline's fantasies.

Caroline set her fork down, her spaghetti plate empty. "What about you? Did you ever have a part-time job?"

Sam took a moment then nodded his head. "I worked for my uncle. He had a small ranch outside of El Paso."

"Ah, so you do know something about this life."

"Well, we had a herd of cattle, but ranching cattle isn't too different. And we had a healthy string of horses, too. Uncle Lee used an old army helicopter he'd salvaged to oversee his ranch. I'd go up in that bird every chance I got."

Caroline could only imagine a young Sam Beaumont completely addicted to flying, watching his uncle fly over the ranch and wishing he was the one behind the controls. "I'm surprised you didn't fly it yourself."

Sam stared down at his plate for a moment, then admitted. "I did. Got my pilot's license when I was twenty."

"You're a pilot?" Stunned, Caroline stared at Sam. Everything she knew in her heart about this man, contradicted his presence here in Hope Wells. Early on, she'd pegged him for a drifter, a man with no ties, no connections to anyone or anyplace, but the man she was coming to know didn't quite fit that bill.

"I was. I don't fly anymore."

"May I ask why?"

Sam glanced at her and for a moment she thought she might get an answer, but then the phone rang. "Oh, excuse me."

Sam watched Caroline answer the phone, twirling the cord on her finger as she leaned against the refrigerator. She smiled as she recognized the caller.

"Hey, Joanie. It's good to hear from you. Yes, yes, I know. I've been busy."

Sam rose from the table and took his plate to the sink.

"A girls' night out? Oh, that's sounds like fun, but I can't. Yes, I know how long it's been since I went out. But you know I've got only the month to get the stables running again. I'm working every day."

Sam put the iced-tea pitcher in the refrigerator, along with the container of Parmesan cheese and Caroline mouthed him a "thank you" as she slid out of his way.

"Yes, I know. I can't use Annabelle as an excuse right now. I do know that, Joanie, but oh—darn. I forgot it's Lucille's birthday. All the girls are going?"

He finished clearing the table, wondering if he should leave rather than eavesdrop on Caroline's phone conversation, but when he looked her way, she put up her index finger asking for one minute.

He leaned against the sink with arms folded and ankles crossed and waited, watching Caroline's eyes dance with delight, her blond ponytail bouncing as she bobbed her head in conversation. He enjoyed looking at her—way too much.

"Okay, Saturday night. You'll pick me up? Great. See you then."

Caroline hung up the phone and walked over to him. "Thanks for helping with clean up."

Sam nodded. "Dinner was good."

"I'm not the greatest cook, but I try."

"You're better than you think."

She appreciated the polite compliment for what it was. "Thank you. Oh, and I guess we're not working all day Saturday like I'd planned. You heard that conversation. I tried, but my friends won't let me off the hook. I'm going out for the first time since…well, doesn't matter. We'll just catch up on Monday."

"I can still work the weekend."

She shook her head. "No, that wouldn't be fair. We'll put in half a day on Saturday and Sunday we'll rest. Remember, we'd agreed on those terms?"

Sam didn't need a day off but Caroline did, whether she knew it or not. He'd agreed to her terms only to seal the deal. He'd worked seven days a week for so long that he really didn't think it a hardship. Although others had, and that's where he'd gone wrong in his life. His priorities had been way off.

He wouldn't make that mistake again.

"Sunday, we rest," Sam agreed.

"Good."

Caroline smiled with warmth in her eyes and she glanced up at the cabinets he'd replaced. "You wouldn't know that these had burned up yesterday. They're so much nicer now with the new doors. You did an amazing job. Have I thanked you properly?"

Sam could think of a dozen ways she might thank him but nothing *proper* entered into his mind. "Twice. You thanked me twice, Caroline," he said, his voice a husky whisper.

"Oh, I did?" She stared into his eyes, her gaze lingering, then she turned and reached up on her tiptoes to put a clean plate onto the shelf. She fumbled, the dish teetering on the edge. Sam moved quickly, sandwiching her between his body and the counter and caught the dish before it crashed. He set the dish on the shelf, fully aware of Caroline's body pressed to his.

He groaned, the sound a hoarse cry of need. He stood rooted to the spot, unable to move away, as his body heated up to a quick sizzle.

"Sam?"

"Shh, don't turn around, Caroline."

But Caroline did just that. She wiggled around, so that she faced him, trapped between his rigid erection and the counter.

Sam closed his eyes.

But her soft voice snapped his eyes open, real quick. "Maybe I need a test of my own."

Caroline leaned in, crushing her breasts against his chest and brought her mouth to his. She kissed him softly, the tender onslaught touching him deep inside. Sam kissed her back with urgency, his body sparked by desire, his mind on complete shutdown.

He swept his tongue in her mouth, his erection grinding into her at the sweet junction of her thighs. She moaned and wrapped her arms around his neck, their lips frantic, their bodies overheated. The steamy kiss lasted a long time, until, breathlessly, both came up for air.

Caroline pulled away slightly, breaking the heated connection. "Wow," she whispered. "I guess I have my answer."

Yeah. *Wow.*

Sam hadn't felt this alive in months, but he wouldn't rejoice. He didn't want the feeling. He didn't welcome the pulsating in his body and the racing of his heart. He stepped away from her, rubbing the back of his neck.

Leaning against the counter, Caroline folded her arms, pushing up breasts that Sam ached to touch as she stared into his eyes. Sam recalled her I-need-a-man statement and wondered if that hadn't been a Freudian slip. A shudder coursed through his body. Caroline was a widow with a small daughter to raise. Sam had had a taste of that life once and had failed miserably. He wasn't the man for Caroline Portman.

"Honey, the way I see it," Sam began gently, "we have one month to get your place up and running. We can work or we can…*play*. Either way, in one month's time, I'm gone."

Caroline's baby-blue eyes grew wide. She blinked back her surprise. Sam had shocked her. Hell, he'd shocked himself. But he had to lay his cards on the table, knowing what was most important to both of them.

Quietly, she confessed. "You're right. I've already had one man run out on me. And it took me a long time to recover. I'm not willing to chance it again. Renovating Belle Star is all that matters now." She smiled and her eyes softened with appreciation. "Thank you for your honesty."

Honesty? Hell, if he'd been truly up-front with her, he would have told her how he wanted to lift her up on that counter and drive his body into hers until they were breathless and sapped of energy.

That would have been the honest truth.

"I'd better go." Sam headed for the door and at the last minute he turned to face her squarely. "Just for the record, don't think it's easy for me to walk out this door."

Caroline bit down on her lip and nodded then she called out just before he stepped out the door, "Sam?"

She had his attention.

"Tomorrow, we'll start over. No more tests. Deal?"

He nodded. "Deal."

Sam exited the kitchen, walking out into the night but even the fresh crisp air couldn't obliterate Caroline's sweet scent from his mind. Or the feel of her soft body pressed to his against that counter.

Sam headed for his room and the bed that Caroline had slept in last night.

Suddenly, one month seemed like an eternity.

Caroline donned her one and only party dress, the black lace-trimmed satin that draped low in the back and hugged her hips tightly. She put on matching strappy heels that felt foreign on feet used to work boots. Foreign but so attractive that it made up for the lack of comfort. By the end of the evening, she could be certain her feet would ache like the dickens.

"The price of beauty," she said, repeating her mama's favorite saying, as Caroline stared at her image in her bedroom mirror. She applied a coat of Candy Apple Red lipstick to her lips then blotted.

Just like her mama taught her.

Caroline shouldn't feel guilty about going out with her friends tonight, but she did. After that night in the kitchen, she and Sam had settled down and gotten to business. She couldn't be happier with the results so far. They'd made good progress all week long. While Sam worked on repairing the stables, bolstering up the stalls and reinforcing the exterior, Caroline had tilled the yard, pulling up weeds that had taken firm root.

Both had worked long hours each day, sharing a quiet meal together in the evenings, speaking little. Caroline would catch Sam watching her from time to time, his dark gaze following her every movement. Her heart rang out from the way he looked at her at times, but even through all that she believed they'd developed a good working relationship.

And even though she felt a sense of accomplishment for the week's work, she still experienced deep-rooted guilt for going out tonight. She missed Annabelle something fierce for one thing and she hadn't forgotten the heat of Sam's kisses the other night.

Her best friend, Maddie Walker, newly married to one of Hope Wells's last remaining bachelors had sized her up perfectly with one wise statement, "Caroline, you've simply forgotten how to have fun."

Well, Caroline decided she did need a little fun in her life. And as Maddie had pointed out, *she deserved it.*

So she set her mind on forgetting about Sam Beaumont and chucking her guilt, at least for one night.

Because tonight, Caroline Portman was doing the town.

Saturday night at Tie-One-On wasn't the place to go for peace and quiet. Sam should have known better, but after a hard day of work, despite Caroline's efforts to curtail him, then catching a good long glimpse of her sliding into her friend's car for a night on the town, Sam had needed a drink.

While he sat at a corner table, three women had approached him on separate occasions, no doubt hoping to lend comfort to a lonely man. Sam politely refused, not being interested. So he'd gotten up to stand against the wall. With beer in hand, he faced the dance floor, blending in with a boisterous crowd.

Past midnight, he was on his third and final beer,

when a group of five young women walked in, laughing and having a good old time. But only one stood out. Only one held his attention.

Caroline.

She wore a knockout black dress that exposed long shapely legs. Her hair was a mass of blond waves and her baby blues, dancing with laughter, were the prettiest he'd ever seen.

She was a knockout and the only woman on earth who appealed to him.

She was his boss, he told himself. The woman was strictly off limits. They'd already settled that. Only trouble was, he wasn't sure he believed it anymore.

He stood, gripping his beer bottle tightly as he watched her dance with some duded-up guy wearing a Stetson. They danced three times, before Caroline begged off and headed back to her friends standing by the bar.

She laughed at something one of her friends said, then turned her head his way. That's when she spotted him. Through the crowd, their eyes met.

An electrifying jolt shot straight through him, his body tightened up, his heart did somersaults. She looked so pretty standing there with dim smoky light casting shadows on her golden hair, wearing a dimpled smile that appeared wholesome and tempting all at the same time. He stared straight into her eyes, the magnetic pull drawing him in.

And she stared back. Slowly, and with what appeared to be a shaky hand, she set the glass she held down onto the bar, keeping her eyes trained on him. He read so much in those pretty blue eyes, a hunger that matched his own, the hot sizzling promise of what was to come.

The attraction was real, sharp and potent.

Mesmerized, he focused his full attention on her and his body reacted, growing hard and tight quickly. With his gaze locked to hers, he took a step away from the wall. The Stetson guy approached her again and she broke their connection. He witnessed her shake her head no, but the guy didn't get the message. Instead, he grabbed her hand and tugged, attempting to get her back onto the dance floor.

Sam was there instantly, gripping the guy's hand, removing it from hers. Sam looked into Caroline's eyes. "The lady's with me."

"I don't think so, pal," the guy said without hesitation. He yanked his arm free of Sam's grip.

Sam ignored him, and faced his new boss, giving her the option. "Caroline?"

Caroline glanced at the other man and confirmed his pronouncement with no apology. "I'm with him."

The guy shoved his Stetson low on his head, cast Sam an angry look then took off mumbling curse words under his breath.

Sam took both of Caroline's hands in his. Leaning in, he whispered in her ear, "Let's get outta here."

Caroline nodded, her gaze never leaving his. She made a quick stop to whisper something to one of her friends, grabbed her purse, then waved farewell to them all. "Bye, ladies."

Sam didn't wait around to hear their stunned

comments. He led Caroline outside and swung around to the back of the building. Leaning his back to the wall, he pulled her against him. Caroline flowed into his arms.

He kissed her immediately, sweeping his tongue into her mouth, tasting her, open-mouthed and frenzied, the fire inside him burning with white-hot intensity.

She moaned and he pulled her in tighter, pressing her into his erection. "You've got me wound up real tight, honey. It's not my usual style, but the Cactus Inn's just next door. It's a nice place and I've got protect—"

Caroline silenced him with a quick kiss. Then she smiled. "Yes."

Sam kissed her back then took her hand leading her to the Cactus Inn Motel. He blocked out all the reasons they shouldn't be doing this, shoved aside all of his misgivings, but he wasn't fooling himself.

Sam knew they were heading for trouble.

And there wasn't one damn thing he could do about it.

Four

Caroline stood inside the neat and tidy motel room, her heart beating like mad. She peered at the no-nonsense furniture before casting her gaze on the queen-sized bed looming before her. She heard the decided click of the door as Sam came up from behind, wrapping his arms around her belly, gently pulling her against him. She leaned back, relishing his heady scent, the maleness of it all and the way their bodies seemed to fit together so perfectly, even in this position. "Why do you still have this room?" she asked as it suddenly dawned on her that Sam had been living in her makeshift guest room for several days now.

"I'm paid up for the month," he whispered, his breath warm against her cheek. "Didn't think I'd see this room again though."

"I didn't think I'd be here either," she said, turning

in his arms to face him. "I don't do…I mean this isn't me. I'm not good at—"

Sam shushed her with a deep lingering kiss that nearly buckled her knees. "I know what kind of woman you are, Caroline, and that's why I'm giving you a way out. Things got pretty hot and heavy back there. You need time to take a step back and think about this because, no matter what happens here tonight, I'm leaving Hope Wells in one month's time. Once the job is finished, I'm moving on."

Caroline understood that. She wouldn't ask for anything more. For too many years now, she'd kept herself in a safe cocoon, wrapped up in making a happy home for her daughter, unwilling to break loose to take a chance on anyone, or on life. She was a single mother who'd been granted this one opportunity, this one time, when she answered to no one but herself. And if Caroline had to indulge in her fantasies, who better to do it with but the only man she'd met in years who stopped her heart? Sam was that man. Though she had questions about him, the why and how of his drifting from town to town, she wouldn't dwell on that now.

Now, all she wanted was to feel womanly again. To be held and loved by a man who seemed to appreciate her. The fact that he'd just offered her a way out when she witnessed desire burning in his eyes, felt it in the way his stiff body pressed against hers, told her more than she needed to know about him.

She slipped the thin black straps off her shoulders in answer. "One month, Sam. You've made yourself clear."

"And you're okay with this…with us?" Sam asked,

and the hope registering in his eyes was enough to boost Caroline's fragile ego.

She nodded. And smiled. Then proceeded to wiggle the rest of the way out of her slinky, special-occasion dress. As long as she was indulging in her fantasies…

She stood before him in a lacy black bra and panties feeling self-conscious and more than a little brazen in her two-inch strappy heels.

Sam took half a step back, his eyes darkening to coal as they scoured every inch of her.

He reached up to stroke through her golden hair, bringing the waves forward to rest over her shoulders and the groan that escaped his throat went deep and guttural. "This is going to happen fast," he said, slowly removing his shirt, button by button, his eyes never leaving her body. His well-paced actions seem to belie his words. "The first time, I mean."

Caroline gulped, staring at the broad expanse of his chest. "The first time?"

Sam grinned and stepped closer. "We have all night."

Rapid hot tremors passed through her body. She breathed out, "Yes. Yes, we do." Oh, she thought, if only he was half as good as he looked, her fantasy would be unrivaled.

"Put your hands on me, darlin'," he said, and before Caroline could react, Sam reached for her hands, placing them to his chest. She laid her palms full out on the solid wall of muscle, feeling every bit of him she could reach. The contact made him groan and pull her into a tight embrace. He crushed his lips to hers, dipped his tongue into her mouth and stroked her with precision.

Caroline reacted in kind, making little throaty sounds as their tongues wreaked havoc on each other. Sam reached around and cupped her buttocks, drawing her closer, so that her softness crushed into his rock-hard shaft.

From there, Caroline lost all sense of time and space. Clothes flew off as the pair landed with a thud onto the bed and rolled until both were satisfied with the position. Sam guided her hands once again, this time to his waist and she toyed with his edge of his jeans until he grunted a complaint, then with a bedeviled smile, she lowered his zipper. He kicked off his boots, and tossed his jeans off in rapid succession, replacing her hands, right where they'd been.

Under Sam's guidance, she stroked him, sliding over the slick surface of his manhood and he moved in her rhythm, their bodies in line and fully tuned to each other. The need was urgent, their mouths hungry, their bodies hungrier. For Caroline, it had been too many years of abstinence. Too long for a young woman with a lot to give. So she gave to Sam, heartily and hungrily and soon, it was his turn to give. He rolled her over onto her back, his legs positioning her with firm command and when he slid his fingers between her thighs, stroking fast, she went slick and wet immediately.

"You ready for me, darlin'? Cause I'm about to implode."

Caroline nodded, too wrapped up in the heady sensations to speak. Heart beating wildly, she slithered up higher on the bed and welcomed him. Within moments, condom in place, he entered her, his full thick shaft filling her body. She ached a little, in a good way, in a way she'd never ached before, and when he began to move, Caroline threw her head back, giving him full access.

His movements were those of a man with need. Fast, precise, controlled, but oh, so incredibly, painstakingly gentle. Caroline moved with him, rocking with his rhythm, their desire seeming equal, what both wanted and needed at the moment. The motel room echoed with their quick, spontaneous, unabashed cries of release.

Sated in a way she'd never been before, Caroline sighed silently inside, a deep purr of satisfaction. Sam lay beside her and when both had caught their breath, he took her hand, entwined their fingers and leaned over to kiss her tenderly. "You're a beautiful woman, Caroline Portman."

Caroline looked up into Sam's deep dark eyes and saw something there that touched her heart. Gratitude. She heard it in the tone and timbre of his whispered words as well and she knew she wasn't mistaken.

She reached up to touch his face, the day-old stubble feeling rough against her fingers. Already, in just a few days, she'd gotten accustomed to him, his face, his rare smile and, now, his body.

If Sam had been grateful, then Caroline experienced that emotion doubly for the act of intimacy they'd just shared. Caroline had never felt more like a woman. She'd never been so aroused, so caught up in the moment. She'd never been so bold, either. She should be covering her face in shame for the audacious way she'd behaved, but she didn't feel anything remotely shameful. How could she when gorgeous, sexy Sam Beaumont was staring at her as though she was a gift he wanted to unwrap again and again?

"Sam," she began, but couldn't bring herself to thank him in words. "It was wonderful."

Sam chuckled, bringing her closer and folding her into his arms. "Not gonna deny that, but like I said, next time we'll take it slow. That's if you want a next time?"

Sam stroked her arms, sliding his hands up and down, then cupped her breast, feeling the weight, his fingers smoothing over her skin like a silken glove. "Please tell me you want a next time," he whispered in her ear.

"I'm ready when you are," she whispered back, already aroused again by Sam's caresses.

He let out a small hoarse cough. "Give me a minute, darlin'" he said, with good humor. "I need some time to regroup."

"Oh, I didn't mean right now. I mean, I did, but not if you're not—"

"Shh," Sam said, "let's just close our eyes a while. It's late and we have the rest of the night."

Caroline mentally chastised herself for not having a clue about any of this. But when Sam tugged her closer, resting her head on his chest, all of Caroline's doubts vanished. She let go of her insecurities and relished just being here with him. And when she closed her eyes she found precious peace in Sam Beaumont's arms.

* * *

Caroline woke from a deep sleep and for a moment, she became slightly disoriented. Where was she? The room didn't appear at all familiar. The bed, the walls, everything seemed strange.

And then she remembered.

It hadn't taken long for the sweet memories of making love to Sam Beaumont in his motel room to resurface. She smiled, stretched her arms full out then let them fall with a contented sigh. Dawn had yet to break through the darkness. She lay beside Sam, his body lending warmth and comfort. Caroline was in bed with Sam having her very first…what? *Affair* seemed too crude a word for what they'd shared. And this wasn't permanent. It was a…fling? Caroline shook her head, no. She wasn't a woman to have flings. Whatever it was, she decided simply to enjoy her time with Sam. No regrets. No repercussions. She faced facts. Once Belle Star was up and running, they'd go their separate ways. And that was okay with Caroline.

So, if she weren't having an affair, or a fling, she'd just have to label this as widow-gone-wild. She chuckled and decided that going wild felt real good. And if she were lucky enough to have Sam's full attention for one month's time, then she'd take it.

She'd indulge in her fantasy. "It's about time," she spoke aloud, forgetting that there was anyone else in the room. Old widow habits dying hard.

Sam cradled her from behind and wrapped his arm around her waist. His touch sparked immediate desire. "You waiting up for me, darlin'?"

Yes. "No, just thinking out loud. Sorry if I woke you."

"You didn't."

Caroline liked the intimacy of being held by Sam, having his whispered words caress her ears, so she didn't turn to face him to respond. She simply relished waking up in his embrace. "Good."

"I'm all rested now," he said in a slow languid drawl that would surely melt ice.

"Are you?" Caroline bit down on her lip to keep from chuckling. She liked playing Sam's game.

"Yeah, I'm feeling pretty…healthy."

"That's good, Sam."

"Yeah, and just so you know…I don't do this…I mean it's been a long time for me."

Caroline found that hard to believe. Sam was too sexy and virile a man not to have ample experience with women. A drifter, a man alone, looking as fine as any one man could get? It seemed to Caroline that women would flock to him. "Well, you certainly haven't forgotten anything."

Sam stroked her hip, making tiny circles with his fingers. "No complaints then?"

"Oh," she gasped as his fingers moved upwards on her torso. "None." She shook her head. "None at all."

Sam lifted her hair, moving it off her neck and planted tiny kisses there, his lips gentle, like a soft breeze blowing by. "Good."

"What…um, what about you?"

"You're kidding, right?" he responded immediately. His fingers found the hollow just under her breast.

He moved with soft caresses until the skin there prickled. Caroline sucked in oxygen. Shivers crept up her belly while heat flowed below. "I'm not fishing for compliments, but I want to know."

Sam stroked her nipple with his thumb, making her ache deep down inside. His body against hers went tight and his shaft hard. "Caroline, a man couldn't ask for anything more."

His admission helped heal past hurts and Caroline secretly thanked heaven for bringing this man into her life for the time being. Maybe that had been the plan all along. Maybe Caroline had been waiting for someone like Sam Beaumont to come along to put a salve on her open wounds.

No more words were spoken that night. And as Sam had promised when they made love again, it was long and slow and as delicious as steaming hot fudge melting over vanilla ice cream.

"I thought Sundays were meant for rest," Caroline cooed softly, her warm naked body pressed against him. Sam kissed her lips, stroking his hands up and down her arms, her creamy skin coming alive under his palms.

They'd left the motel at 6:00 a.m., Caroline keeping a low profile. Sam wanted it that way. He knew how judgmental small towns could be, and he wasn't sure how many people had noticed them striding out of Tie-One-On last night, barely able to keep their hands off each other, but he had to try to protect her. He wanted to leave Caroline with her reputation intact and her stables workable again.

But as soon as they reached her home, they'd reached for each other again and wound up horizontal on her bed. Sam hadn't experienced lust like this before. Not even as a young military recruit in his early twenties, or when he'd first married his wife, Lydia, had he felt this kind of raw elemental need. He chalked it up to self-imposed celibacy and the lonely months of drifting. But he knew one thing for sure—at this rate, they'd never get any work done.

"That's what we're doing. Resting."

"*Now,* we're resting," Caroline said with a dimpled smile. "But what happened a few minutes ago I would label as an intense workout."

"You made the rules, boss lady. Sundays we rest. Seems we've defined *resting* in new terms, though."

Caroline moved away from him enough to look into his eyes. She looked so beautiful right now, all soft and dewy-eyed, like a woman who'd been sexually sated. Sam wanted her again. Seemed he couldn't quite get enough. It took a great deal of self-control to keep from pulling her into his arms again and staking claim to her body.

"Sam, do you think that if we don't work, we'll end up doing this all day?"

Sam chuckled. "All day? Now, that's a tall order, but I think I'm up for the challenge."

Caroline's pretty mouth dropped open. "That's not what I meant. I guess…I don't know what I mean. It's just that, I've never…oh, you know. It's never been so—"

"Hot?"

She nodded.

"Good?"

She nodded.

"Amazing?"

Caroline shoved at Sam's chest, pulling away from him. "Don't tease me."

"I'm not. If you put your hand below my waist, you'll see that I'm serious as hell."

Caroline swallowed. And to his amazement, she did just that. She touched him under the sheets. The heat of his arousal sizzled in her palm. A groan escaped from deep inside his throat.

"Oh, Sam. What's gotten into us?"

"You might want to amend your 'Sundays we rest' policy, darlin'."

"Yeah, I think you're right. Shall we get up? I'll fix coffee, and we'll get some work done today."

Sam covered her hand with his, so that her grip on him intensified. "Don't think I can just now. Coffee can wait."

Sam encouraged her with gentle kisses and softly spoken words, until she moved once again with heat and passion beneath him. He needed her one more time, before he could concentrate on any work today. Caroline seemed to be in tune with him, generously offering what Sam so desperately craved. He came up over her, their eyes connecting, their bodies already familiar with each other, and as he entered her once again, thrusting gently, taking her with him, he marveled at Caroline's giving nature, the way she trusted him so completely.

He stroked her breasts, palming the deeply darkened circles as they peaked pebble-hard. Gasps of pleasure sprang from her lips, her face awash with such intense satisfaction that Sam's body reacted in kind. He brought them to the brink quickly then, showering her with escalating thrusts that lifted them higher and higher.

The release called to them both, each in their own worlds, then they came together in their fall back down to earth.

Sam lay sated and complete upon the bed, his face turned up, staring at the ceiling. "Can I say I think you're amazing, without you thinking I'm teasing?"

Caroline purred beside him.

"And beautiful." He turned to face her. "So beautiful, Caroline."

She smiled at the compliment, then stroked his chest, her fingers playing with the curling hairs there. "I think I could stay here all day, after all."

Sam grasped her hand and, bringing it up to his lips, he kissed her knuckles. "Yeah, a tempting offer, boss lady, but we have work to do."

He'd promised to help Caroline refurbish her stables so that she could have that grand opening she'd spoken about with such excitement. She had a deadline, and so did he. He wouldn't stay in Hope Wells longer than one month, so he might as well get cracking. There were stables to rebuild, a yard that needed tender, loving care and fences to mend. He kicked off the sheets and got out of bed. And when he turned to find Caroline's pretty blue eyes on him, her blond hair spread across the pillow, her sheet-clad body partially exposed, he knew he'd never seen a more stunning woman in his life.

But as his gaze wandered off slightly to the night-stand beside the bed, a photo he hadn't yet noticed caught his attention. A cherubic face, with blue eyes and curly locks, stared up at him, the child's face full of joy and expectation. Sam's heart slammed hard with regret and gut-wrenching pain. He'd almost forgotten. For the past twelve hours, Caroline had consumed him, mind, body and soul. But along with Caroline, came a beauty of a child, so much like his own Tess, that he couldn't bear to look any longer.

"Sam, what's wrong?" Caroline asked.

Sam smiled, transforming his grief-stricken face. He shook off her question. "Nothing. I'm going to take a shower."

He left Caroline's room as old and wearisome grief reminded him of why he was drifting, why he could never go back to the life he'd once led. Of why he'd leave Hope Wells in his dust in a few short weeks.

Five

Maddie Brooks Walker stared out Caroline's kitchen window, her gaze following the movements of the man upon the roof of the larger of the two stables on the property. "You say Chuck at Tie-One-On vouched for him?"

Caroline nodded and sipped from the tall glass of lemonade she was enjoying with her best and newly pregnant friend. "Yep. Chuck said they spent time together in the military, years ago."

Maddie frowned. "He doesn't look…I don't know. I hate to judge, but he's not your typical handyman."

Caroline grinned, thinking back on the last ten days and nights she'd spent with Sam. He wasn't 'typical' in any way, shape or form. From the way he worked with his hands, so expertly, so precisely that he seemed to craft the stables, fixing and repairing with the smallest amount of effort and the greatest amount of knowledge, to the way he worked his hands on her, so magically with gentle touches and hungry caresses that calmed her and heated her all at the same time. "All I know is that he's good at everything he does."

Maddie turned sharply to stare into her eyes. It must have been the tone of her voice, the way she spoke of Sam that put suspicion in her best friend's eyes. "*Everything* he does?"

Caroline smiled, turning away to pour more lemonade into both of their glasses.

Maddie walked over to the kitchen table, her gaze never leaving Caroline's. "Tell me."

Caroline sat down. Maddie did the same. A just-missed car accident on the main street of town a few years back had the two women bonding a friendship that would last until both were grandmothers. The pretty young veterinarian had fallen in love with the most stubborn, hard-nosed, best-looking bachelor in Hope Wells, and with a little help from Caroline and others, Trey Walker had finally realized that Maddie had been meant for him all along.

Caroline cherished their friendship. She wouldn't lie to Maddie. But these past ten days with Sam had been heaven, so private, so intimate. During the day, they'd work their fingers to the bone on Belle Star and at night, they'd fall into bed together and make love. And on those nights when one or both were too exhausted, they simply lay in each other's arms until sleep claimed them.

For Caroline, it was her fantasy come true.

She was living her dream, rebuilding her stables and sharing her nights with an incredible lover.

No regrets.

No repercussions.

Caroline granted herself these blissful weeks before motherhood and her professional life would once again claim her. "He's…very good."

Maddie leaned in, her green eyes rounding on her. "So you've said. How good?"

Caroline sipped lemonade. She'd never make the same mistakes she'd made with Gil. Her judgment and objectivity had been way off the charts then, but Caroline knew what she was getting into with Sam. She had no qualms about what she was doing, but she didn't want Maddie to worry about her. "He's very—"

"If you say *good* one more time—"

"Gentle, Maddie. Caring. And passionate. Just what I need, right now." She didn't add "sexy as sin." She guessed that Maddie had figured that out.

"Okay," Maddie said with a little pause, "got it. I would never judge you, honey, but are you sure you know what you're doing?"

"I've never been more sure. Sam's here to help out with Belle Star. He's hired for one month and he's been a godsend to me."

"Oh, dear. That's what I was afraid of. What if he decides to move on?"

Caroline smiled and with a shake of her head, she said, "That's exactly what will happen. And I'm okay with that. I won't fool myself into thinking he'll stick around. He's a drifter and I know that. Once the stables are done and Annabelle comes back, he'll be gone. I won't ever allow myself to get so caught up with emotion that I'm blinded again. Gil's negligence nearly destroyed Annabelle's legacy. He nearly destroyed me. My heart's well-protected now. I have no illusions."

Caroline stared out the window, watching Sam hammer the roofing material onto the top of the stables, his hair slicked back, his T-shirt sticking to his skin, exposing a strong and vital physique. "This time, I'm in control of my own destiny. And *you*, my dear pregnant friend, have nothing to worry about. Just concentrate on that new little baby growing inside you. How's Trey doing with all this?"

Maddie took one last glance out the window, looking at Sam, seeming unsure whether to let the subject drop. Then, with a sigh, she focused on Caroline, one hand placed on her still-flat belly. "Well, Trey's nervous, excited, crazed and thrilled. We both are. We can't wait. And he's looking at me differently now. Like he's afraid I'm going to break or something. It's really kinda sweet."

Caroline chuckled. "I can just picture that. Trey—the confirmed bachelor, happily married now and entering into fatherhood. Who would have guessed that ever happening a few years ago? Good thing you came to town when you did. Trey's life would have been much different if he hadn't fallen for you."

"Yes, it's amazing how fate works, isn't it?"

"Yes, in your case, amazing." Caroline maintained her smile for her best friend. She wouldn't relay her own disappointment when fate hadn't turned a kind hand toward her. She'd never been granted that wonderful kind of doting attention when she'd been pregnant with Annabelle. Gil hadn't been thrilled. He hadn't done anything to make her feel special. His indifference to the joyous occasion of their conceiving a child should have been a clue. There had been so many clues. And she'd labeled herself a fool for not recognizing all the signs earlier. No, fate hadn't been kind to her in that regard. But she had hit the lottery in bearing a beautiful daughter. Everything she did now was for her daughter's sake.

"How's our little Annabelle doing in Florida?" Maddie asked.

The mention of Annabelle always brought a smile. "I miss her terribly. I have to hear her voice at least once before I can get to sleep at night. So, Mom and Dad make sure we talk every day. She's being spoiled, I'm sure. But I can't even work up any real worry over it. That little girl deserves all the attention she gets. Lord knows, she didn't get much from her own father."

Caroline closed her eyes momentarily then shook her head. "I'm sorry. I shouldn't have said that."

"It's okay, Caroline. You can speak the truth with me." With that, Maddie rose from the table. She glanced out the window once again. Caroline followed the direction of her gaze and both viewed Sam Beaumont, shirtless now, at the base of the ladder, gulping water from a liter bottle. "I'm not going to judge you in any way," she added, with a little wink. "I'm glad you're making progress here."

Caroline appreciated Maddie's undoubting support

and loyalty. She knew she could trust her friend and loved her all the more for it. "Thanks. Things are going really well. I'm hopeful that I'll have my grand opening as planned." Caroline glanced at Sam again, before reassuring her friend. "I've got my eyes wide open this time."

Maddie gave her a hug. "Good thing, too. Because he's an eyeful."

"Maddie!"

Maddie grinned. "I'm pregnant, not blind. Oh, and don't exhaust yourself with all the *work*."

"The work isn't what's exhausting me," she said and both women laughed. Caroline walked Maddie outside. "I still have my maternity clothes. You're welcome to all of them, if you'd like. Just let me know when and I'll gather them up for you."

"Thanks," Maddie said, getting into her truck and starting the engine. "That's one offer I can't refuse."

Caroline waved until Maddie was out of sight on the road. She turned and bumped right into Sam. Moist with sweat, sun-baked to a golden brown, his body glistened. "What if I make an offer *you* can't refuse?"

Caroline smiled into his hungry eyes, her heartbeats racing. "What would that be?"

"Take a shower with me."

Water rained down, the steam rising up and over the shower door, bringing with it the fresh scent of soap. Caroline hesitated just outside the fogged-up pane, watching the silhouette of Sam Beamount as he lathered up his body, a body she'd come to know intimately.

She'd never showered with a man before. This was a first. Sam had introduced her to many firsts.

She stood there naked, biting her lip, wondering, with a sexy man waiting for her, why she hesitated. And a fleeting thought burned through her mind, a thought that frightened her. She was becoming accustomed to having Sam around. She liked seeing him in her kitchen in the morning. She liked sharing a cup of coffee and the day's work with him.

She liked him. Period.

And now, seeing him in her shower and enjoying the sight of him there…meant something. She recalled her words to Maddie earlier, words spoken from the heart. Sam was here only temporarily and Caroline had no illusions about him staying on. But now she wondered at her own bravado. Had she'd fooled herself into believing that Sam could leave here, leave her and then she'd go about her daily business, safely tucking away the memories of the times they've shared? Could she bank all recollection of her *first* shower with a sexy, passionate man and move on with her life?

"Hey," Sam said, opening the shower door slightly, granting her a peek at his wet slick body, "you coming in, darlin'?" He reached for her hand.

Caroline sighed before taking his hand. She shoved those niggling thoughts aside and accepted his hand. "I'm coming in."

"Good, 'cause it was getting lonely in here." Sam moved her to the back of the tiled shower wall, pressing his body to hers. Without a moment's notice, his lips were on hers, his tongue going deep into her mouth. Her breasts crushed into his chest, her thighs rubbed with his, their legs, rough to smooth, entwined. Though he protected her from the stream of hot water, his moisture became hers and soon she was as slick and wet as Sam.

"I should dock your pay for this," she murmured, after the long passionate kiss ended.

Sam stroked her breasts with one hand, while the other found a different playground, down past her waist. "Fine by me, but I think after this, you'll be wanting to give me a raise."

"No way…oh!" Caroline gasped as he cupped her between the thighs, stroking that sensitive spot until her body moved on its own accord. The sensations ripped through her as she gyrated to the rhythm of his stroking. He kissed away her tiny moans then went on bended knee to replace his fingers with his mouth.

Caroline rocked back from the jolt of pleasure. He gripped her hips to steady her and continued his assault. She closed her eyes. Water rained down on both of them, bathing them with steam and heat. She moved faster now, locking her fingers in Sam's hair, holding him to her as she lifted higher and higher, the cold wet tile from behind her brace. Sweet sensations gripped her, electrifying jolts that spiraled her into a world all her own.

"So…good, Sam." Caroline barely heard her own murmurs.

"Stay with me, darlin'. There's more."

Caroline hung on tightly, her body wracked with pleasure.

Sam lifted up then, kissing her gently, allowing her time to come down slightly. Then he spun her around. She faced the stream of water now and he moved her closer so that her face was protected from the onslaught. The shower of heat and spray paraded down her hair and back. Sam wove his fingers in her hair, toying with the tresses, kissing her throat, her shoulders and back from behind.

His shaft nudged her thighs and she felt the thick massive erection readying for her. With slick moist hands, Sam positioned her, guiding her hands above the faucets and bending her slightly at the hips. He braced his hands there and moved with her, teasing her with thrusts and caresses that touched and tempted her womanhood.

Sam's breaths came faster now, his thrusts harder.

The new position created sizzling tingles that spiraled into hot tremors. She wanted Sam with a desire she'd never known before. But before they'd really even begun, Sam spun her around again and turned the shower off.

Caroline stared at him, her mind whirling, her body humming.

"We need protection," he whispered with regret, "before this gets out of control."

Caroline had forgotten all about protecting herself. She'd forgotten everything but the man standing before her and the passion he'd elicited from her, a passion that could easily spin out without restraint. Good thing Sam hadn't forgotten.

No, of course he wouldn't forget. For whatever his reasons, he had an agenda and nothing would deter him from that. She knew him to be honorable enough not to leave her high and dry and pregnant. No, Sam, her temporary lover, wouldn't want the complication of a child.

He towel-wrapped her quickly and lifted her into his arms. "We're not quite done," he said, carrying her out of the shower.

Caroline had a momentary lapse. They seemed to be coming more often now. Her fantasy man was taking up too much space in her head. She found herself thinking about what life would be like if Sam Beaumont decided to stay in Hope Wells permanently. The rational part of her brain warned her not to fall for Sam; she had a mission in life and he was only the means to the end. Building Belle Star was all that mattered. Still, a small part of Caroline wished that he wouldn't leave at all.

But once he laid her down on the bed, all thoughts flew out of her head. Sam bent to her, kissing her lips, stroking her body and, now fully protected, he rose above her and entered her. The familiar warmth healed what hurt Caroline deep inside, obliterating all thoughts but the here and now.

Caroline moved with him, his thick shaft filling her, absorbing her heat as they climbed, thrust after thrust to the ultimate peak. Caroline's release came fast and urgently and she felt her body's completion from her head down to her toes. Sam wasn't far behind. And when they both lay sated and spent on the bed, she turned to look at him.

He smiled then touched a finger to her cheek.

Caroline smiled back. "I guess I won't dock your pay after all," she said.

Sam's expression changed, his eyes downcast. He glanced away from her for a moment, then when he turned back to look at her he opened his mouth to speak. "Caroline…" was all he managed.

She sensed what he had to tell her was somewhat important, urgent maybe. "What is it, Sam?"

Sam glanced above her head, seeming to focus on Annabelle's picture on her nightstand for a brief second before turning away. "It's nothing."

Caroline held her breath. "I think it might be something."

Sam rose from the bed granting her a great view of his powerful body. "I plan on working into the night."

"Sam, I was just kidding about docking your pay."

Sam shook his head. "Damn it, Caroline. I know that. But there's a helluva lot more work to be done and I have less than three weeks."

Nineteen days to be exact. "We're on schedule."

"You have to be ahead of schedule. In case something comes up that you hadn't planned."

"Like what?"

"Like, I don't know…anything." He lifted his arms in frustration. "A storm that will delay our work. Or an injury. Or someone not coming through with supplies."

Caroline sat up on the rumpled bed, looking at Sam now with deep interest. "Who are you, Sam?"

Sam glanced at Annabelle's picture one more time then turned his attention to her. "Just a man who's trying to keep his promise."

Three afternoons later, Sam flipped open his cell phone on the first ring and sidestepped into the stable, out of Caroline's range of vision. Only one person knew the number. Only one person would call him. And Sam hadn't spoken with his brother since before coming to Hope Wells. "Hey, Wade," he said.

"It's been more than a month."

Wade wasn't happy. Sam couldn't help that. He'd always been close to his younger brother. He cared about him and loved him. He was probably the only living breathing person that Sam did love.

"You promised to call once a month."

"I lost track of time."

"What the hell are you doing?"

Sam smiled as he glanced out of the stable to find Caroline admiring the new sign she'd had specially made for Belle Star, complete with burned-out wood lettering and a long length of golden stars outlining the perimeter. Sam had lent a hand in the design, but all in all, it was Caroline's baby. She'd known exactly what she wanted, and now that the deliveryman had deposited the large gate sign near her front steps, she stared at it in awe.

Sam's smile broadened. He admired her drive and gumption. Hell, in truth, there wasn't a darn thing about Caroline Portman he didn't admire.

"You still there?"

Wade's irritation came through loud and clear. "I'm here. I'm fine, Wade. Sorry I missed our deadline."

"Yeah, well, that's exactly what I need to know. That you're not lying *dead* somewhere. You took off eight months ago, big brother. Our father's fit to be tied. He's got men out looking for you."

"You've told him that I'm okay, right? And I don't want to be found."

"About a hundred times. But the old man doesn't like being left in the lurch."

"I should have left the company years ago." Sam couldn't say the words that remained stuck in his head. Words that he lived by. Words that he couldn't forget.

If I'd left the Triple B, Tess would still be alive today.

Gnawing guilt ate at him every time he allowed himself to think about the driving force that had led him astray. He'd wanted to prove his worth, to earn his father's love. It wasn't until Tess died that he'd realized his father was incapable of real love. The old man had only one true passion in his life—the Triple B. The construction company that he'd nurtured and fed with all his heart was Blake Beaumont's only love.

When he'd been too *busy* to attend his granddaughter's funeral, showing up hours later at the house, Sam had finally figured it out. He'd wasted his entire life trying to gain the love and respect of a man who had no heart. Sam had thrown him out of the house that day. And then he'd taken off shortly after, relinquishing all of his responsibilities, all of his duties at the Triple B.

He wanted no part of Blake Beaumont. He feared he'd become just like him. For Sam, there'd been no other way. He'd had to leave. To run away.

But Sam didn't think he'd ever really recover.

The running was what he needed to stay sane.

"You gonna tell me where you are?" Wade asked. Sam had expected this. Wade asked the same question every time they spoke.

"Nope. Not necessary."

"You don't trust me?"

"It's not a matter of trust." Sam couldn't explain that he needed the anonymity; he needed a complete, one-hundred-percent break from his old life. Not even Wade would understand that entirely.

"I'll call you in a few weeks. There's no need to worry."

"Don't miss your deadline again, big brother."

Sam chuckled. Wade acted like an old mother hen. He hadn't seen this side of his carefree brother before. He knew Wade missed him. Sam felt the same. But he couldn't face coming home. Not even to see his brother. "I promise. I'll call early this time. Hey, I miss you."

Wade hesitated before answering with heavy emotion. "Yeah, same here. Take care of yourself, Sam."

Sam flipped off the phone and glanced outside the stable, his gaze darting around the perimeter of the grounds until he located Caroline. He locked on to her image as immediate fear coursed through his system. "Ah, hell!"

He took off running, hoping to get to Caroline before disaster struck.

Six

Caroline had promised Sam that she'd wait for him to hang the sign but from the moment she'd seen it, with carved-out lettering and brilliant golden stars, she knew she had to be the one, the *only* one to place the sign where it rightfully belonged. It was fitting somehow.

Belle Star Stables was hers. And Annabelle's.

And the sign signified all that she'd accomplished so far. It signified what was to come. It held promise to the future. Maybe Caroline was being a bit melodramatic, but she didn't care. In her heart, she knew that she had to hook that sign above the gate to Belle Star all by herself.

By sheer determination and stubborn will, she managed to drag the heavy sign to its place beneath the gate. Then with all her might, she managed to heave the sign up the ladder, pulling it up from behind as she climbed the rungs. When she reached as far as she needed to go, she turned, trying to maneuver the heavy plank. She wobbled, the ladder shook, but she managed to lift the sign over her head, hooking the left side. She lost her balance then and the sign swung down like a swiftly moving pendulum. Caroline reached for the swinging sign, grabbing it just before it knocked into the ladder. "Whoa, that was close," she murmured.

With one side hooked firmly, Caroline reached way over, stretched as far as she could and somehow managed to hook the right side. The sign hung proudly now, but she'd reached just a tad too far over and the ladder swayed. Caroline did the same trying to keep her balance, but all she managed to do was to kick out from the ladder's rungs.

Luck wasn't with her.

The ladder fell one way and Caroline toppled the other.

"Caroline!" Sam's urgent voice resonated in her head.

She fell to the ground with a hard thump.

Sam hadn't reached her in time.

He caught the ladder instead, the wooden rungs trapping him to the ground beside her.

He stared at her with concern.

She gazed up at the sign, swinging slightly in the breeze. She'd done it. She'd hung the sign all on her own. There was something uniquely significant in that.

She smiled and murmured, "Isn't it beautiful?"

Sunlight faded to black, the gate sign the last image Caroline viewed before her eyes closed.

* * *

Sam paced and paced, his mind reeling. It had been three hours since Caroline's fall from the ladder and he still couldn't quite resign himself to the notion that she'd be okay. He'd stood outside her bedroom for a long time, peering in from the hallway on occasion, allowing the doctor and a set of friends who'd heard about her mishap to lend her comfort. It never ceased to amaze him how quickly word traveled in a small town.

Sam had acted quickly, dialing for help, refusing to move Caroline into the house until the paramedics showed up on the property. He didn't know the extent of her injuries and wouldn't chance moving her. But she'd woken up minutes later, demanding to get up and continue with her chores. It was all he could do to keep her down and calm enough until help arrived. She'd absolutely refused to be taken to the hospital. Sam figured both her pride and her lack of decent health insurance had caused that reaction.

So the town doctor had come out and examined her. No serious injuries. None. Thank God. But she did suffer a mild concussion from the fall.

Sam paced some more.

He didn't like the feelings emerging in his gut. Anger boiled over at her stupidity. Why in hell had she decided to hang that sign without his help? And the panic he'd felt once he'd realized he couldn't get to her in time brought out old and painful wounds of his own.

He'd been damn scared seeing her topple from the

ladder, but the fear inside him was nothing compared to his overwhelming concern. He cared about Caroline.

Perhaps too much.

A nasty buzzing in his head wouldn't relent.

He didn't want to care about anyone. Not ever again. And here he was, worried about Caroline Portman as if she had a place in his life.

She didn't.

Sam wouldn't go down that road again. Not ever.

"You can go in to check on her now," a uniformed man who had previously introduced himself as Sheriff Jack Walker announced. "She's feeling better," he said with relief.

Sam studied the man who had proclaimed a long-term friendship with Caroline. He'd spent the past half hour inside her room, holding her hand, making her laugh. Sam hadn't liked the sharp fleeting pangs he'd encountered seeing her smiling at the tall good-looking sheriff.

"That's good," Sam said.

"Yeah, Caroline's a keeper. I wouldn't want to see her get hurt again." Sheriff Walker spoke kindly enough, but the rise of one eyebrow told him the man might have meant something entirely different.

"I'll make sure she rests."

Walker eyed him thoughtfully. "Maddie's going to come out to stay with her tonight. My cousin's new wife won't have it any other way. Seems Caroline needs to stay awake throughout the night."

"That's a good idea." Though Sam's initial instincts were to stay by Caroline's side tonight, it would be better this way. Distancing himself from her a little would help get his feelings in check. The last thing he needed was to fall for Caroline. And he was absolutely certain Caroline would be better off without him. He had no place in her life. He wasn't a family kind of man.

"Sam, are you out there?" Caroline's soft sweet voice called to him.

"Seems he's been pacing off the design in your rug," Sheriff Walker announced, sticking his head inside the door, "waiting to see you."

Sam pushed past the sheriff. He strode into the room and his heart stopped for a moment, seeing Caroline looking exhausted, her face so pale that her beautiful blue eyes looked like deep dark troubled waters. She lay propped up in her bed with two pillows beneath her head. "I should wring your neck."

Sheriff Jack strode into the room, taking a place beside him. "Now that's what I call real tender loving care. You want I should toss him out?" He winked at Caroline, making her smile again.

Sam wasn't in a good mood, and the tall lawman was beginning to gnaw at his nerves.

"It's okay, Jack. I can handle Sam."

The sheriff chuckled. "No doubt about it. See you on Saturday night, then?"

Caroline glanced at Sam with what appeared to be guilt. "Maybe. No promises."

Sam glared at the sheriff. He'd definitely overstayed his welcome and when the lawman finally took his leave, it wasn't soon enough for Sam.

Caroline watched her friend exit the room before turning her full attention on him. "I think you mentioned something about wringing my neck?"

Sam crossed the distance to her bed. He sat down carefully and chose his words with extra thought. There was no sense upsetting her now. Her head must ache like the devil. "We were going to hang that sign together. What made you change your mind?"

"It was something I needed to do myself." She shrugged it off. "I'm not sorry I did it. But I'm sorry that I caused all this trouble."

Sam nodded. Oddly, he understood that need. Hanging that gate sign was symbolic, speaking of Caroline's much-coveted independence and her sheer determination to restore the stables to their rightful place. But he wouldn't condone Caroline putting herself in danger. "Seems you've got a core of friends who worry about you. I've met at least five of them today."

"Yes, well, that's a small town for you."

"I'd say you're one lucky woman."

Caroline stared into his eyes, her lips lifting ever so slightly. He wanted to plant tiny gentle kisses there until both needed more. He'd miss sleeping with her tonight, even though he knew that they wouldn't make love. He had a need to hold her to reassure himself that she was safe and unharmed.

"I'm lucky because I have friends, or because the fall didn't take me out?"

"Neither. You're one lucky woman because I decided not to wring your neck after all."

Sam bent over, kissed her quickly on the lips and exited the room. Her friend would be here soon and Sam had double the chores to do now. But he didn't mind. Working kept his mind off Caroline and the subtle ways in which she was beginning to break down all of his defenses.

Sam spent the rest of the afternoon working on the stables, priming the outside of the wood siding for paint. He'd replaced many of the old planks, where weather, age and neglect had damaged a good percentage of the outside walls. He'd spoken with Caroline about saving time and money by simply using a protective coat of varnish for the outer walls, but she'd insisted on painting the stables the same creamy light-beige color that matched the house, complete with chocolate-brown trim. The appearance of the grounds had to be impeccable. It was something she wouldn't negotiate. Which meant more time and energy spent on the exterior.

There was still a good deal of work to do on the interior of the stalls and Sam had a good handle on improvements inside that would save Caroline and her helpers a lot of work, once the stables were up and running.

As it was now, at full capacity, both buildings could house twenty horses. The monthly revenue provided by boarders would ensure Caroline a steady income, and any added features, such as supplying riding lessons and opening up a small tack store could definitely increase her profits. But it was hard work for a woman alone with just some part-time help.

Sam intended to make her job as easy as possible before he left Belle Star. He slapped on the primer, watching the color absorb into the wood, as rambling thoughts filtered into his head.

Who the hell was Sheriff Jack Walker anyway? And had he asked Caroline on a date?

See you Saturday night then?

Sam knew he had no claim on Caroline. It shouldn't matter that she'd been asked out for Saturday night. The cocky sheriff made no bones in showing interest in her. And Sam wouldn't do anything to embarrass Caroline or himself in front of her friend Jack.

Sam couldn't name what his relationship with Caroline was, exactly. He honestly didn't know. In the beginning it had seemed like a good idea. They'd been up-front with each other. There seemed to be an undeniable attraction that they both wanted to satisfy. Sam hadn't deceived her. She knew he'd leave in a month. Caroline seemed fine with that.

All of his instincts told him that Caroline Portman wasn't the dallying kind of woman. She didn't have much experience with men, or in having affairs. Sam had known that about her the minute she'd walked up to him at the bar with her proposition.

So, why had it bothered him so much that Jack Walker could make her smile?

Sam continued slapping on the primer with a vengeance. He worked fast, making his way around the corner of the building. He had turned to work the back of the structure, when something in the distance caught his eye.

He set down the paint and brush and walked over to a small tricycle in obvious need of repair. The handle was tweaked in such a way that it couldn't be ridden anymore.

Sam bent down, his heart hammering in his chest. He placed his hand on the small triangular seat, caressing it and imagining the young excited rider. Though he knew the tricycle to be Annabelle's, another image popped into his head.

"Watch me, Daddy! Watch me ride." Tess looked up at him with eager eyes, so proud of her accomplishments on her new trike. Sam sat down on the front lawn of his Houston house as his three-year-old daughter began to pedal, her little legs working hard, her hair blowing in the breeze, her face alight with joy. "See me, Daddy."

"I see you, Tess," he called out, right before his cell phone rang.

The call had come in due to an emergency on site. The foreman at the Triple B had been injured and Blake Beaumont insisted Sam take over the project. "We need you there, boy. Right now."

Sam took one last look at his daughter riding down the sidewalk before taking off for that high-rise building project. He hadn't returned until late that night and he entered Tess's room immediately.

She opened her eyes, looking so terribly sad. "You didn't see me, Daddy. You didn't."

"I did, Tess. I saw you ride your new trike, sweetheart."

But Tess had turned away then, closing her eyes, pretending sleep.

Sam stared at the broken tricycle for long moments, his heart aching. He'd been such a fool. He'd lost the most precious gift a man could ever hope to have, and for what, to gain the respect and love of a man incapable of either emotion?

Sam's wife had left him shortly after that, taking Tess along. But for their daughter's sake, they'd made allowances, pretending to be one big happy family whenever they were together. Sam missed Tess in his daily life, but by that time, he didn't know how to fix things. He'd neglected his wife and child for the sake of the company one too many times.

And the last time he'd let them down they'd paid dearly, with their lives.

"Sam?"

A pleasant-sounding voice interrupted his thoughts. He lifted up from the tricycle and turned to find a pretty red-headed woman smiling at him.

"I found you," she said. "Hope you weren't hiding from me."

"Ah, no. I didn't know you were looking for me."

"Caroline sent me out on a mission. Hi. I'm Maddie Walker." She put out her small delicate hand. "The town veterinarian and Caroline's good friend."

Sam shook her hand. "Sam Beaumont. Is anything wrong? How's Caroline feeling?" Sam moved away from her then to peer around the building, glancing toward the house. "Does she need anything?"

Maddie shook her head. "Nope, not a thing. She's doing fine. Talking my ear off about Belle Star."

Sam nodded, hiding his relief.

"But she's worried about you."

"Me?"

"Have you eaten anything?"

"No, but I won't starve. There's nothing for her to worry about."

"It's past eight. The sun's almost gone. Why don't you come inside? I brought over a tamale casserole. It sure would ease her mind if you had some dinner."

Maddie looked at him and he instantly knew that she'd been informed about his relationship with Caroline. But there was no judgment in her eyes, only concern.

"She cares about you, Sam."

He muttered a soft curse. He didn't want this…this caring. He'd spent the better part of the year blocking out those feelings.

Maddie turned and walked away. "I'll tell her you'll be in after you clean up."

"Right," he said to her back.

Sam walked over to the tricycle, taking one last look before picking up his paint supplies. After stowing them away, he headed to check on Dumpling. Soon the horse would have loads of company, but right now, the gentle mare had only him.

And tonight, all Sam had was the mare.

He found comfort in that.

And later that night, Sam retired to the guest room in the back of the stables unable to work up an appetite. He had some thinking to do and tamale casserole inside Caroline's cozy kitchen didn't fit into his plans.

* * *

"Should you be up?" Sam asked, as Caroline walked toward the stable Sam had been priming last night. She brought out a steaming cup of coffee as morning sun worked its way through low-lying gray clouds. The air was hot and humid and she wondered if she should have forgotten the coffee in favor of something cold and refreshing.

"I'm feeling better. Maddie took great care of me. She left about half an hour ago."

"Yeah, I saw her take off in her truck."

"She had an emergency across the county. A stray dog was hit by a car."

Sam winced. "Bad?"

Caroline lifted a shoulder. "I'm not sure, but if anyone can fix the injured, it's my friend, Maddie."

Sam took the offered coffee from her hand. "Well, then it's a good thing that she stayed with you last night."

Caroline smiled then looked at the work he'd done on the stable. "Maddie said you were up before dawn, painting." Caroline admired his work. "You've gotten a lot accomplished already. I'll change into my painting clothes and join you. We should finish this building by the end of the day."

"No."

"No?" Caroline looked into Sam's dark brooding eyes. His jaw set, he didn't move a muscle. "You don't think we can finish or—"

"Or, I think you need to take it easy today. I can finish this on my own."

"I have work to do, Sam. I'm not going to let a little setback stop me."

"Caroline, how much sleep did you get last night?"

She rolled her eyes. "You know the answer to that. Maddie stayed over so that I wouldn't sleep much. She roused me every few hours. But I'm feeling fine. Great actually. And I'm anxious to get back to work."

"Fine, then, why don't you go inside and work out the budget for the supplies we're going to need. I'll make a trip into town tomorrow once you've worked it all out."

"Sam." Caroline didn't want to pull rank. In her heart she knew that Sam was only trying to help. But she'd been run roughshod over by the best of them, and she'd vowed never again. No man, not even sexy Sam Beaumont was going to tell her what to do. "I'm perfectly capable of taking care of myself. The budget is all done anyway, and it looks like if we don't get cracking soon, a summer shower might just take the chance from us. I promise to stop when I get tired."

Sam grunted, taking a sip of his coffee then setting it down to give her a sideways glance. "You're the boss."

Damn straight, she wanted to say, but she smiled instead and within minutes she was painting the lower half of the stable, while Sam worked up on a ladder, painting the upper half.

By the end of the day, they'd nearly finished the entire building. Only the trim remained.

"Not too shabby for amateurs," she said, once they'd cleaned up their paintbrushes and put everything away. Satisfied with the progress they'd made, she leaned against the corral post adjacent to the stable, working the kinks out of her shoulders and neck. Everything ached, including her bones. She was totally wiped out, but couldn't confess as much to Sam. He had an I-told-you-so look about him right now as he studied her, with his hands planted on his hips. Even through paint smudges on his face and clothes, the man looked like heaven and if she weren't totally exhausted, she might have wanted to do something about it.

"You need a hot bath," he said. And just as she was about protest that he wasn't looking all too clean either, he finished with, "and a massage."

Caroline closed her eyes at the thought. Was that a legitimate offer? Because she would surely accept. Nothing sounded more perfect. "Mmm."

"No extra charge for the service, ma'am. Then a quick supper and I'm tucking you into bed."

"Sounds…interesting." She raised her brows.

"Alone." Sam's expression didn't change. He appeared dead serious. "You need a good night's sleep."

Caroline surmised that Sam Beaumont was accustomed to barking orders. She'd certainly seen it firsthand. Ever since she'd taken that fall from the ladder, he'd somehow taken control. Caroline had more experience now and she knew that she would pick her battles wisely.

On the one hand she was touched by his concern, but more importantly, she wouldn't have another man telling her how she felt and what she should do about it. Caroline had grown up through hard knocks and harder lessons. She'd learned to trust her own instincts, so if Sam wanted to dictate orders then he had a stubborn opponent on his hands. She had a few surprises of her own. If all went well, her man Friday wouldn't know what hit him.

She smiled at his comment about sleeping alone tonight. Softly, she added, "We'll see."

His plan was to let Caroline get the rest she needed tonight. No way had Sam expected to sleep with her. She'd been injured and had hardly slept the night before, then she'd stubbornly insisted on working alongside him until fatigue took the sparkle from her pretty blue eyes. Offering her a massage hadn't been in his plans, either. It would be much harder to say goodnight and retire to his guest room that way. But he'd seen how her body stiffened up after they'd finished work for the day. He'd imagined the soreness settling into her bones and the weariness she must have felt.

Hell, massaging her tired body seemed like a real good idea at the time.

But as he stood outside her bathroom, listening to her contented sighs with each little splash of water, Sam knew it would be a test of his willpower to keep from making love to her tonight. He wanted her. That was a given. But he wanted her to rest even more. And a part of him wanted to make sure he wasn't getting in too deep. For both their sakes, Sam had to keep it simple so that when the job was finished here, he could walk away without looking back.

Caroline opened the door wearing a smile and not

much else but a fluffy towel that barely covered her female assets. "I'm ready for my massage now." Her smile was bright, the sparkle returning to her eyes. "Where do you want me?"

Sam took a swallow. *Where did he want her?* On a soft cushion of straw out in the stable. Out in the tall green pasture as the sun began its decline. On the kitchen table. "How about on your bed?"

Caroline smiled. "I'm looking forward to this." She brushed past him, heading to her room. The soft scents of flowers and freshness followed her. Sam did, too.

He cleared his throat. "Yeah, well, I'm not an expert at this, so don't expect much, okay?"

She turned her head, her eyes full of mischief. "Anything you do to me will be just fine, Sam. I've never had a massage before."

Sam opened his mouth to debate the issue, but clamped his lips shut instead. His body kicked into overdrive and he had a hard-on developing that only Caroline Portman seemed capable of inspiring.

Out of nowhere it seemed Caroline handed him a bottle of body oil. Then she lay down on her belly, and wiggled her toes. "I'm ready when you are."

Sam stared at her back, the towel dipping low now, barely covering her sweet little derriere. Sam had seen the woman naked before, but this time, it was different somehow. More exciting. Definitely sexier than anything they'd yet encountered. And the open trusting way in which she offered herself up to him gave him pause.

"I read once that massaging the body releases endorphins. They called them the happy hormones. Well, Sam, honey. I'm ready to get happy."

Sam chuckled. He poured oil onto his hands, rubbed it in then came down gently on her shoulders.

"Ohhh," she cooed with pleasure as his fingers worked deeply into her skin. He felt the knots unwind slowly as her body released pent-up tension. He surmised the release wasn't just from a hard day's work today, but maybe from months and months of doubt and worry about her future. She'd taken on a whole lot lately and as he worked kinks and tightness from her smooth skin, he hoped to erase past pressures and concerns as well. "Feel good?"

"Mmm, you don't know how good."

But Sam knew. She might be the recipient of the massage, but Sam's body was feeling good right about now, too. He closed his eyes and absorbed her softness. His hands slid over her shoulders and with each little moan of pleasure she murmured, Sam's body reacted in kind. Giving her pleasure brought him pleasure.

And pain.

He worked lower on her back, pressing his palms firmly onto the triangular area just above her derriere. His fingers fumbled when he got too close, causing Caroline to giggle. "It's okay. I'm sore there, too."

Sam sucked in a breath. "Hell, darlin', a man can only take so much."

For his own sanity, he skipped over those two lovely mounds of flesh, still covered by the towel he noted thankfully, and began working on her upper thighs. He slipped his hands up and down, taking in the creamy firmness, rubbing oil in and working the tension out.

He moved down past the backs of her knees, caressing the lower legs, stroking his palms up the long length and down again. With every delighted sound Caroline made, Sam's body grew tighter. Her flowery clean scent invaded his nostrils and the dewy softness of her skin under his palms caused his undeniable hard-on to strain against the material of his jeans.

But he pressed on, back up to knead her shoulders then he worked his hands up and down her arms, emitting happy hormones along the way. When he entwined his fingers with hers, sliding them in and out, for just one moment, Caroline grasped his hands still. They remained locked for several beats, both bodies frozen momentarily as unspoken words traveled between them.

Sam's heart ached, but his wounds still ran deep and he couldn't allow Caroline in. Not in that way.

God, not ever.

Sam leaned over her, whispering in her ear. "I'll go heat up the tamales. You must be hungry."

Caroline rolled over, the towel now unfastened and exposing the most beautiful woman Sam had ever seen. "I'm not hungry for tamales, Sam."

She handed him the body oil. "There's more to do."

Sam hadn't an ounce of willpower left. He'd commended himself on keeping his sanity during that rubdown, but he wasn't immune to Caroline, as he'd once hoped. Hell, he'd rather cut off his right arm than leave this bedroom now.

"I need you, Sam," Caroline whispered.

Sam needed her, too. And that's what scared him. He didn't just want Caroline Portman. He *needed* her.

And that need churned inside him. She was an ache that wouldn't go away. A pain that seared his gut and wrecked his mind.

Sam hadn't intended to make love to Caroline tonight. He'd wanted to keep things simple. It was essential to his survival. But right now, taking her in his arms seemed more essential and he couldn't fight his desire for her another second.

He dripped oil onto her breasts, each little drop hitting its mark, until Caroline's eyelids lowered and tiny gasps escaped her throat. "Oh, Sam," she whimpered.

Sam massaged the oil in, caressing her full round globes until heat nearly sizzled from her skin. Then he bent his head and licked the tips with his tongue until her gasps grew louder. He dripped oil everywhere and the massage took on new meaning as she gyrated to his every touch, moved to each of his caresses.

Sam stripped off his clothes and returned to her, fisting her long blond locks in his hand while he crushed his lips to hers in a long passionate kiss. "We're both gonna get happy now, darlin'."

And when Sam entered her with one powerful thrust, her eyes rounded. She breathed in deeply and accepted him fully. He moved inside her with almost violent need and Caroline didn't rebel, but caught up to his rhythm, racing with him now, and when their explosion came both rocked for long lingering moments, the release something shattering and all-consuming.

Sam stayed inside Caroline a long time, their bodies meshed, their arms and legs tangled. Both needed the comfort, the connection. When their breathing finally steadied, Caroline whispered, "You're good for me, Sam Beaumont."

Sam rolled off her then and stared up at the ceiling.

He couldn't respond, and if that hurt Caroline, he was painfully sorry.

Because he knew he wasn't good for Caroline.

She was dead wrong.

Seven

The scent of brewing coffee woke Caroline from her sleep, the aroma teasing her nostrils and tempting her to get out of bed. She opened her eyes as daylight poured into the room. Caroline smiled. Her body rejuvenated from Sam's expert hands, she couldn't remember a time when she'd felt so contented and so incredibly free.

She rose and showered quickly, putting on a pair of jeans and a white tank top. When she entered the kitchen, Sam looked up from sipping coffee at the table, his eyes noting her appearance and lingering on the silver writing stretching across her top: Cowgirl Up.

"Nice," he said and her temperature shot straight up. Sam had a way of looking at her that told her just what he was thinking. And sometimes, those hot hungry looks made her blush. Then he added with curiosity, "Too nice for painting."

Caroline poured herself a cup of coffee and stood across the table from him. "That's because I don't intend on painting until later in the day. I've got to make a trip into town and run some errands. I'll pick up the rest of the supplies we need at the lumberyard. We're down to our last ounce of coffee beans and there's not a thing in the house to eat."

"I'll finish up the painting. We got a lot accomplished yesterday. I should have it done by the time you get back."

"Actually, I have a favor to ask of you."

Sam sipped his coffee and watched her over the rim of the cup he held. "Another massage?"

Once again he'd made her blush. That sensual massage would be in her head for years to come. And the way he'd taken her last night, as though his life depended on it, wasn't going anywhere either, that memory was imprinted for all eternity.

"No, nothing like that."

Sam smiled. "Too bad."

"I'll take a rain check though."

"Any time, darlin'. What's the favor?"

"I need a ride into Midland on Saturday."

"What's in Midland?"

"The Lone Star Horse Rescue. I'm hoping to adopt a pony for Annabelle. I want it to be a surprise when she comes home."

"She's a little young, don't you think?"

Caroline sat down on the chair facing Sam. She settled in, tucking one leg under the other. "I know. But I think it would be good for her. When we open the stables, I'll be busy with all the horses and I don't want her to feel neglected. This way, with a pony of her own, she won't feel left out. I'll make sure I spend time with her, teaching her how to care for it."

Sam studied her a moment, his eyes unreadable. "You're a great mother, Caroline."

Caroline leaned way back in the chair. Almost speechless, she managed, "Thank you."

It was probably the kindest, most generous compliment he could have given her. Caroline tried, but she wasn't perfect. She knew she'd made mistakes in the past, but being a good mother to Annabelle was her number-one top priority. Such easy words, but somehow coming from Sam, they meant a great deal.

"So we're off to Midland tomorrow," he said.

"It's just a preliminary interview. These adoptions can get pretty intense. They'll go over all my applications to make the final determination. I won't know for some time if I'm accepted or not. But it's worth the trouble to adopt a good animal in need of a home."

"I can't imagine them not approving you."

"Maddie will vouch for me and they'll go over my resources and the facility to make sure I'm capable of caring properly for the animal. I'm hoping to be approved." She shrugged. "I could drive into Midland myself, but I guess I need the moral support."

"You've got it. We'll get an early start in the morning.

I'll have to get you back in time for your date with the bumbling sheriff."

"The bumbling sheriff?" Caroline laughed. "Oh, you mean Jack? Good lord, Sam. I'm not dating Jack. How can you think that?"

"He asked you out right in front of me the other day."

"Yes, and you think that I'd date someone, after…after what we've—"

"Caroline, no. I didn't think that. But I wasn't sure what to think."

"Sam, I've known Jack Walker since I was a kid—a really little kid. Our parents were good friends and he's like a brother to me now. He offered me a ride to Maddie and Trey's monthly poker game. The game is sort of a tradition in the Walker household and since Maddie came on the scene they include the ladies once in a while. I told Jack I'm not going."

"You could go. I mean…you and I…we're keeping it simple, right?"

Caroline planted her feet on the ground, pushed out her chair until it squeaked against the wood floor and stood up. "Right. *Simple.*" Caroline cocked her head to one side, her thoughts in turmoil. "Maybe I will go after all. And maybe I'll call Jack back and ask him to pick me up."

Sam pushed out from the table too and rose abruptly. "Okay, never mind. So, it's not simple. Truth is, I don't want you anywhere near that guy. And I have no right to feel that way and even less of a right demanding that of you."

Caroline looked into his eyes. Again, Sam had surprised her with his open, honest admission. She'd known the stakes when she'd slept with him.

One month.

And then he'd be gone.

She forced herself to realize that Sam had no claim on her. And she had no claim on him. She didn't fully understand why he had to leave in one month or why he'd put himself on such a deadline. She figured it was better that she didn't know. His leaving was inevitable. But he was here now and she wanted to make the best of it. "You don't have to demand anything of me, Sam. I don't want to go out with Jack. That's *simple* enough, isn't it?"

Sam nodded, but his gaze held hers. "Simple and a whole lot of complicated."

Caroline dropped the subject before she said something she'd regret. She wanted no regrets with Sam. Neither could she afford them. "I'd better get going. I want to get back in time to get some work done."

Sam looked her squarely in the eyes. "I want to take you to dinner tomorrow night, Caroline."

Stunned, she asked, "Like a real date?"

He nodded.

"You think that's wise?"

"Hell, no. But you deserve to be taken out. Saturday night is date night, isn't it?"

With a slow nod, she agreed.

"I'm asking, and I'm hoping you'll accept."

Caroline sent him a smile. "I accept."

Her heart ached for what could never be, but she

vowed to make the best of this situation. And she couldn't think of a better way to spend her Saturday night.

"Good then," Sam said. "It's an official date."

And there was nothing *simple* about it.

Sam finished painting the stable in the early afternoon, the second coat going on faster than the first. He had to admit that Caroline had been right. The difference between the freshly painted stable and the one yet to be painted was incredible. No amount of varnish would have made the stable look so elegant. The clean fresh look of the stable would certainly instill confidence and entice serious boarders. There was no doubt in his mind that Caroline would take the best care of the horses left in her charge.

After he'd cleaned and tucked away all the equipment, he took a long hot shower, scouring off all remnants of paint, then dressed in a clean pair of jeans and a chambray work shirt. He thought he'd saddle up the gentle mare and take Dumpling for a ride to inspect the fences surrounding Caroline's property.

He knew there were repairs to be made, but he wanted to mark the damaged areas so that he could estimate the cost and supplies needed first. And he had to speak with Caroline about ways to make the inside of the stables more durable. He had a few ideas on the subject.

Sam exited the bathroom and looked across the hall. The door to Annabelle's room was open and bright little-girl colors caught his eye. He'd never ventured down the hall before, wanting to keep his distance, which wasn't hard to do since Caroline tended to keep the door closed most of the time.

But today, the vivid colors drew him closer and as he approached, a copper-haired doll with big blue eyes and a wide smile beckoned him.

He recognized the doll; it was named Patsy Pumpkin. He'd given one just like it to Tess.

And though he knew better, he continued on down the hall until he found himself inside the room surrounded by soft fluffy animals, crayon drawings and the sweet angelic scents of childhood.

Pinks and lavenders, brilliant yellows and neon greens colored the walls and small furniture. Sam leaned over the bed, picking up the doll from her perch atop a purple chenille pillow. He held the doll away from him, clutching her tight as memories rushed in.

Tess, hugging the doll to her chest.

Tess, playing in a room not at all so different from this one.

Tess, falling asleep without a kiss from her daddy.

How many nights had he missed tucking her into bed?

"I'm sorry, honey," he whispered, shaking his head slowly. Tears that he'd never allowed welled up in his eyes now. Emotions he usually tucked within the confines of his mind surfaced with unyielding bitter clarity. Sam welcomed them. He deserved the heartfelt anguish. He'd been a terrible, neglectful father. "I'll never forgive myself, Tess. Not ever."

"Sam?"

Caroline's curious voice startled him. He remained where he stood, holding Annabelle's doll.

And when Caroline moved into the room to look at him, Sam couldn't meet her eyes. He spoke softly, "I've never come in here before. Didn't think I could face it."

"Sam?" Caroline said again. He couldn't miss the concern in her voice. "What is it?"

Sam sank down on the bed, staring at the doll he held. "I had a daughter once. She would have been Annabelle's age, had she lived."

Caroline's soft gasp didn't surprise him. Parents weren't supposed to bury their children. "Oh, Sam."

She lowered down beside him on the bed. "I'm so sorry. How did it happen?"

Sam continued to stare into the eyes of the doll as the confession rolled off his tongue. "A helicopter crash. It was my fault."

"Oh." Again, he heard Caroline's soft intake of breath. Most people weren't used to hearing these kinds of confessions. Sam knew he'd staggered her.

"It's not what you're thinking. I didn't fly the helicopter that day. I should have. I should have been there to fly my daughter to her grandparents' house. My wife's…my wife's family adored her. It was Tess's birthday and she was so excited to be visiting them. But I was too busy. An emergency came up at work. I had to postpone the trip. Tess had been heartbroken and my wife had had it with me disappointing our daughter. I can't say that I blame her. I let Tess down time and again. And this was her birthday celebration.

"Lydia had already left me by then. But we held it together for Tess's sake whenever we could. She was so angry with me she hired a pilot and took Tess on that helicopter with her. The weather turned bad and the pilot was inexperienced. They all died in that crash."

Caroline touched his arm. "Sam, I'm so sorry. But it wasn't your fault. You didn't cause that crash."

Sam turned to her, unable to hide his pain. "Don't, Caroline. Don't try to make it easy for me. I'm to blame. I neglected my daughter countless times. I should have piloted that chopper that day. I know they'd all be alive today if I had."

"You don't know that for sure, Sam," she said softly.

She'd repeated his brother Wade's words exactly. But he'd tell her what he'd told Wade and everyone else who'd tried to ease his guilt. He'd tell her what he knew in his heart to be true. "I know, Caroline. That pilot made mistakes only a rookie would make. If I'd been flying that day, the crash wouldn't have happened. I should have been there."

"So, now you don't fly anymore?"

"Not once since then."

"Oh, Sam."

Sam rose from the bed. "I shouldn't have come in here."

Caroline stood to face him. "You need time to heal, Sam. And to forgive yourself."

Sam shook his head, the pain inside burning raw and deep. He'd never spoken of this before today. He'd held it all inside. But with Caroline...he felt she would understand. And although he unleashed the burden of his guilt to her, he didn't feel any differently. Nothing could change his self-loathing. No one would ever know the depth of his own self-contempt. "I'll never forgive myself, Caroline."

Caroline stood frozen to the spot, shocked by what she'd just heard. The pain in Sam's voice, the anguish on his face, the grief he couldn't let go tore at her heart. She loved Annabelle with her very soul. She couldn't imagine losing her. Any parent would feel the same. So Caroline understood Sam's agony. She understood his guilt.

Of all of her wild imaginings about the mysterious, quiet-spoken drifter, this wasn't what she'd expected. His admission had certainly answered some of her questions, but the brief glimpse he'd given her into his life had also provoked even more questions. He'd been married. He'd had a wife and child once. Where had they lived? And who was Sam Beaumont, exactly?

Caroline saw the depth of pain in his eyes, heard it in the defeated huskiness of his voice. She knew she'd never ask those questions, but she hoped that maybe Sam would open up to her more about himself one day.

Self-protective devices told her to let it be. Not knowing about Sam would save her heartache when he left. But Caroline wasn't made that way. She'd never protected herself to the point of not caring about another human being. She hadn't built up that tall a wall of defense.

She took Patsy Pumpkin with her and closed Annabelle's door. Caroline walked into the kitchen, peering outside the window in time to see Sam saddle up

Dumpling then mount her. With a black Stetson on his head, his body rigid, his face a mask of stone, he headed out on the mare. She watched until he became a faded silhouette on the horizon.

Caroline clutched the doll to her chest. Her stomach ached. Her heart broke in two. Her eyes filled with tears. She knew Sam's pain. It matched her own.

Because Caroline realized in that one moment that she'd fallen in love.

Eight

The drive to Midland was quiet, Sam making only light conversation. Caroline sat in the passenger seat of his truck with a file folder on her lap containing all the pertinent papers required by the Lone Star Horse Rescue for the pony Caroline hoped to adopt. She realized how this might affect Sam. Up until yesterday, she had no reason to worry or concern herself about Sam's feelings regarding doing anything for her child.

But now that she knew, she wondered how hard this must be for him, helping her surprise Annabelle when she returned from Florida. He hadn't flinched when she'd asked, Sam had always given her his full support.

He'd been unselfish with his time and had worked so hard at Belle Star that Caroline loved him even more for his sacrifice.

That she loved him at all had come as a shocking revelation. She'd thought herself immune to love, thinking her failed marriage to Gil had destroyed all hope for a happily ever after. Not that she'd hope for that with Sam. She had a better understanding of him now. She suspected his reason for drifting from town to town had to do with his daughter's death. Perhaps he was punishing himself. Perhaps he wanted no ties to anyone or any place. Moving on from month to month would afford him that luxury. Perhaps he needed that to survive. To not care. To not feel.

Caroline ached for him. And she wanted him. But she wouldn't delude herself. Sam didn't love her. He might never be capable of the emotion again. Certainly, Caroline hadn't thought she could ever experience love again.

And the shock of it all remained with her.

"It's up ahead, just a few miles. Are you nervous?" Sam asked.

"A little. But I'm excited, too."

Sam reached out to her side of the seat and took her hand in his. He squeezed gently. "They'd be foolish not to approve you."

"Thank you, Sam. It means a lot."

Sam nodded and spoke again, this time more softly as he continued to hold her hand. "About yesterday. I want to thank you for the things you said. It meant a lot to me. But let's move on from there. You don't have to walk on eggshells around me."

"Does that mean you're willing to talk to me about your life?"

He shook his head. "It won't change anything, Caroline. So no, I'm not going to dredge up the past."

Caroline sighed. The pain was still too deep for Sam to open up to her. She understood that. When Gil had abandoned her, it had taken her weeks to admit it to anyone. She'd just "pretend" it away and make excuses for why Gil wasn't home. That only lasted a short time before her friends and neighbors got suspicious.

But Caroline recalled the pain as if it were yesterday. She'd hated Gil for what he'd done to Annabelle. She felt betrayed for herself, but she'd also felt humiliated—a complete failure as a wife.

It had taken her a long time to come to terms with that. And still she wondered about the role she might have played in his abandonment. Still, in a corner of her mind, she'd wondered about her own character flaws that might have sent him packing.

In her heart, she knew that Gil hadn't been right for her. He hadn't been the love of her life. She'd recognized that immediately after they'd wed, but she had loved him in the beginning. She had tried to be a good wife and mother. She'd finally come to the conclusion that Gil was the one with the character flaws. Gil hadn't known how to commit. He hadn't known how to care about anyone but himself.

Caroline had matured enough to realize that now. And she understood Sam better because of it.

"Okay. No dredging up the past."

Sam sent her a charming smile. The first one she'd seen from him since she'd found him in Annabelle's room yesterday. "Thanks."

The smile and gratitude sent her heart into flip-flop mode so she was glad when Sam pulled the truck into the rescue site. "Would you like me to wait or go with you?"

"Oh, I'd love your input on the horses. Maybe we'll find a filly here."

"You got it."

Sam strode beside her and within minutes, Caroline was meeting with the facilitators who explained everything once again in person. She'd already done most of her research by phone calls and the Internet, so what she learned now about the rescue organization wasn't entirely new to her.

She turned in the remainder of her paperwork. Some of her applications were already on file, so she had a little head start there. "Now, that the papers are in order, would you like to see our horses?" Betty Manning, the director asked.

"Yes, please. As you know, I'm looking for a filly or colt. It's for my daughter. And it would be best if they both grow up together."

"Well, we have two to chose from now. One of each gender. Both came to us as foals."

As they walked outside, Caroline caught sight of more than a dozen animals in corrals, grazing peacefully. Some of the horses had obvious physical problems, but for the most part they looked healthy enough and well-cared for.

"It's a misconception that we only rescue and adopt out horses that nobody wants or that aren't healthy enough to sell. Many of our horses are worth thousands of dollars, but their owners would rather see them adopted out to a good home with our strict policies on protection than to put their horse on the selling market. As you know, we take pride in keeping track of the adoptions, and we make sure the horse goes to a loving home."

"Yes, I know. That's one reason I decided on a rescue. Believe me, if I'm approved, the horse will have all the love we have to give."

Betty smiled and nodded. "That's all we want. Ah, here they are." She stopped at a smaller corral, where the two animals were nuzzling and playing with each other. "Striker is our colt. He's the bay. And Princess is our filly. She's the chestnut. Both have come here under different circumstances. Striker's owner died and the family is selling the farm, but decided to send him here since they didn't know enough about the animals to sell them. Princess, well, she's a whole story in itself, but the bottom line is that she survived a horrible mudslide. I won't go into details, but she was a wreck when we first got her. She's healthy now and a great little gal."

Caroline stepped over to the corral fence and called to the animals. Both shied away at first, but then with more coaxing, Princess wandered over. Caroline spoke softly, "That's a girl. You're a survivor, aren't you, girl?"

Sam walked over to where Striker stood. The colt took one look at him then dashed around the corral, snorting and prancing, showing off his talents. Sam chuckled. "This one's feisty. I'd take him in a minute if I could, Caroline. But I think the filly might be better for Annabelle."

"Princess is definitely the more sedate of the two, but neither are going to roll over and play dead. They both have spirit," Betty said.

Just then Princess backed up and pranced off, running circles around the colt.

"Oh, this is so hard. I wish I could adopt them both. They look like standardbreds."

"They are. You know your horses, don't you?" The director said with a hint of admiration. "They're bred to have great ground manners and they adapt to any tack you have available."

"They don't grow too large, do they?"

"About fourteen to sixteen hands. They have longer bodies and shorter legs. Which is perfect for a child."

Caroline nodded and smiled. "Well, I've made up my mind. Princess it is. She'd be perfect for my little girl. Now that my applications are in, how long before I get word?"

"Well, since you've sent some of the work in earlier, I'd say we'd have a decision in a few weeks. We'll give you a call."

"She won't be adopted by anyone else, will she?" Caroline bit her lip. She'd pretty much attached herself to this filly already. She wouldn't want to lose the chance to adopt her.

"Not much chance of that. No one else has filed paperwork for her yet. So, you'd have first consideration."

"Great," she said.

They all shook hands and Betty said her farewell.

Caroline stared at Princess, wanting this so much for

Annabelle. She could only imagine her daughter's face when she laid eyes on Princess and learned that she had her own pony.

Sam sidled up next to her. "You made a good choice, Caroline."

Caroline feigned a shudder. "Now, all I have to do is go home and wait by the phone."

Sam wrapped his arm around both her shoulders and pulled her away from the corral. "C'mon. Let's go into town. I'm starving. And there's some things I want to discuss with you about improving the stables."

"So," Sam said, "what do you think? If you invest the money now, you'll get a lifetime of wear from the stable stalls. The horses you boarded before chewed them down and destroyed a good deal of the wood. With reinforced stalls, they won't get their teeth into the wood as easily."

"I didn't know how badly Gil neglected the horses." Caroline couldn't hide her remorse. She loved animals and hated that she'd been so caught up in keeping the household going when Annabelle was a baby that she hadn't paid enough attention. She should have guessed that Gil would cut corners. He did very little to preserve the stables and the Portman good name. "Many of them turned to cribbing to ease their boredom and frustration and as a result, they ate through a good deal of their stalls," Caroline said, setting her fork down.

She and Sam sat in the shade at an outside café, opting for the peace of outdoor dining and fresh air instead of the noise inside the busy eatery. Sam tackled a grilled cheeseburger, while Caroline chose a chicken salad. A case of nerves had her insides churning and her appetite waning. The past twenty-four hours had made mush of her mind and hammered her stomach to pieces. She'd fallen in love and planned on adopting an animal, and now Sam proposed she spend the bulk of her remaining budget on the interior stalls at Belle Star.

"The horses need exercise every day. And they'll need to be turned out. You have enough grazing land for that right now, but it doesn't mean that when you do stable them, you won't end up with all the same problems."

"I know, Sam. But it's expensive. And right now, I can only afford to repair the broken stalls. Once the stables turn a profit, I can look into rebuilding the stalls."

Sam looked doubtful, his jaw set stubbornly. "What if I—" he began, but then clamped his mouth shut. He stared into her eyes and shook his head. "You're…the…boss."

He seemed reluctant to lose this battle and even more reluctant to speak those last words. He'd held something back, she assumed, something that warred within his mind. Caroline knew he had a good head for business, but she knew precious little else about him.

When the meal was over, they headed to the hardware store to pick up a few supplies before heading back to Hope Wells. Caroline made her purchases quickly and Sam carried everything to the truck, loading the supplies into the back.

"Oh, look at the sweet pup," Caroline said, striding over to a tiny Jack Russell on the street. She was a sucker for animals anyway, but she'd once had her own Jack Russell so the pull was magnetic. Before she knew it, she was speaking to the owner, petting the pup.

Sam leaned against his truck, smiling at her. Caroline was a remarkable woman. He'd always thought so, but the more he'd come to know her, the more he admired her.

It was all he could do to stop from convincing her to let him purchase the new reinforced stalls for her today. In his estimation, he felt she vitally needed them to ensure the success of her stables. And Sam had almost made the offer. But good sense had followed. First, he'd have to tell her who he was and he wasn't ready to do that. He could barely face it himself much less speak of it. He'd already shed part of his soul to her yesterday, and he'd spent the night tossing and turning as old memories crept into his mind.

Secondly, and probably more importantly, she'd never accept his monetary help. She had more pride and guts and determination than most men he knew. He wouldn't insult her. He wouldn't offer something he knew she needed, because she'd have to refuse.

So Sam held back. It would be better for both of them that she not know his real identity. Better, because Sam was getting too close to her, getting too deeply involved.

Knowing that he would leave in less than two weeks was killing him, while at the same time, it was a balm to his soul. It was necessary to leave. He banked on it. But he'd miss her terribly. Still, spending time with a drifter whom she'd never see again and creating won-

derful memories was better than messing up both their
lives with the truth.

"Sam, isn't he adorable?" Caroline came toward him.

Just then, Sam noted two men slowing down their
black SUV on the street near Caroline. The license plate
read: 3B HSTN.

Caroline glanced their way, but to his knowledge,
they hadn't seen him. He waited for them to pass, then
grabbed Caroline's arm and spun her back into the
hardware store. He pressed her against the wall and
watched through the window as the car moved on down
the street.

"Sam?"

Sam blinked and refocused on Caroline.

"What are you do—?"

He kissed her.

His lips claimed hers in a sweeping long kiss that
probably shocked most of the patrons entering the store.

When he ended the kiss, Caroline's brows furrowed.
Out of breath, she asked. "What was that all about?"

"You looked so cute with the puppy. I couldn't resist."

Caroline's mouth twisted. She shoved his chest.
"You're lying through your teeth." She glanced out the
window, searching. "Who were they? And why don't
you want them to see you?"

Sam sighed and kept silent.

"Well?"

Caroline was no fool. Sam had to reassure her. But first
he wanted to get out of town. "C'mon. Let's get going."

Caroline shook her head and crossed her arms over

her middle. She set her chin stubbornly. "No. I'm not going anywhere until you give me some answers."

"What do you want to know?"

"Who are they?"

"I don't honestly know." He didn't know who the men were, but he'd noticed their license plate and it was a Triple B car. He didn't know if they were here on legitimate business or if his father hadn't given up his search for him. Sam had made it clear that he didn't want to be found. But true to his father's style, that didn't seem to matter. Even this, his father had to try to control.

"Then why are you hiding from them?"

"There's a difference between hiding and not wanting to be found."

"No, there's not."

"In my case there is."

She looked at him suspiciously. Sam had to wipe that look from her face. The last thing he wanted was Caroline's mistrust. "I'm not a criminal."

"You're not?"

"No! Of course not."

"Do you owe money?"

Sam chuckled. "No. I don't owe a soul anything."

He could see Caroline's mind working overtime. She wanted the truth. Sam couldn't give it to her. He wasn't ready. "Then why—"

Sam took both of her hands in his. He looked deep into her pretty blue eyes and spoke from his heart. "I need your trust on this. Do you trust me?"

She hesitated. "I did."

"Past tense?"

Caroline searched his eyes, looking for and finding what she seemed to need. She sighed. "No, not past tense. I do trust you."

"Good. Know this, I haven't committed any crime and I'd never hurt you in any way. I know you have questions, but I can't tell you anything more than I have already. Do you think you can live with that?"

"I, uh," She nibbled on her lower lip. Then, she shrugged. "If I have to."

It was asking a lot of her, he knew. But the wall of anonymity he'd created around himself was his only protection. He needed that. And yes, perhaps he was hiding, hoping not to be found out. But he'd give Caroline one last parting bit of information, to help her understand the trust she'd placed in him. "Let's just say it's a family matter."

Under the circumstances Caroline thought it best to cancel her date with Sam tonight, but the man was adamant and wouldn't take no for an answer. She'd been wary and suspicious all afternoon and the debate going on in her head all but wore her out. The very last thing Sam had said to her surrounding the events of this afternoon was that it was a family matter. That eased her mind quite a bit. She'd come to the conclusion that if it was truly just a personal matter between family members then she could live with that. She had to. Sam wouldn't share anything more of his life with her. But that didn't mean she wasn't completely and utterly curious about his family and what had happened that kept him from wanting to be found. She surmised that it was none of her business and left it alone.

So she put the finishing touches on her appearance tonight. Instead of the black dress she'd worn that night at Tie-One-On when Sam had swept her off her feet, she wore a clingy crimson dress that still dangled the price tag, a pair of matching red heeled sandals, chandelier earrings that nearly touched her shoulders and a thin silver necklace that dipped into the hollow between her breasts.

Sam had said to dress up, and this was the best she had. She smiled at herself in the mirror then scooped up her long blond hair, rounding it into a knot at the back of her head and pinning it in place with a shimmering rhinestone clip. Some tendrils escaped, falling loosely around her face and shoulders.

Caroline liked the look and had gone for broke. She knew that Sam would leave soon, her precious Annabelle would return home and the stables would open, with a flourish she hoped, putting her life back into a tailspin. She'd be swamped with everyday chores and life would return to normal. She wanted to embrace tonight's memory, holding nothing back.

When the knock came sharply at seven, Caroline moved to the front door. Usually Sam just wandered in through the back so she wasn't entirely sure what to expect. She opened the door with a quick tug and she could barely keep her mouth from dropping open.

Sam stood there wearing a pair of black pleated

trousers, a gray silk shirt and a matching tie with his suit jacket slung over his shoulder. Groomed to perfection without a hint of a beard and every lock of hair in place, he looked like a million dollars and then some.

Caroline's stomach dipped. She berated herself for agreeing to this date. She should have known better. Sam wouldn't be in her life much longer and seeing him like this only intensified the pain. But she was sick and tired of living her life in fear of feeling something for someone again. She told herself to buck up. To have fun tonight and forget everything but what happened in the moment. And in those fleeting seconds, that's exactly what Caroline decided to do. She put aside her fear and buried her pain. This was her time alone with Sam. She wouldn't think past tonight. Hadn't Sam said that she deserved a night out?

"Wow," she said, stepping back from the door.

Sam walked in and handed her a bouquet of yellow roses. She'd been so floored at seeing him all cleaned up that she hadn't even noticed the flowers that he held. "Thank you," she said, "they're gorgeous."

"No," Sam said, taking her into his arms and planting a light kiss on her lips, crushing the bouquet between them, "*you're* gorgeous, Caroline. The most beautiful woman I've ever known."

Caroline could have melted in a puddle then, her heart singing with joy. "Thank you," she said looking into Sam's serious dark eyes. From the look about him tonight, she knew she wasn't in for a casual date. Sam had *dangerous* written all over him.

"I'll…I'll just put these in water," she said, heading to the kitchen, fumbling with the bouquet like a love-struck teen.

Sam followed, and, as soon as the flowers were standing in a clear cut-glass vase, Sam wrapped his arms around her, nuzzling her neck from behind. "I hate to rush you," he whispered, "but if we don't get out of here now, there's no telling what might happen."

He was close, so close that his body pressed against hers, leaving no room for doubt what he was thinking.

"Sam," she breathed out.

"Shh," he said, nuzzling her neck again. "Mmm, you smell good."

"It's… Sinful."

He groaned. "What's *sinful* is that that kitchen table is looking real good to me right now. But then I'd ruin your pretty red dress, wouldn't I?"

Sweet heat spread through her body. "Wouldn't want to rip my new dress."

Sam contemplated.

"You might scuff my shoes too," she said, deciding to play his game. "When you tossed them off."

He sucked in oxygen. "Right."

"And my hair might come down in a mess of tangles," she said softly.

Sam chuckled and whipped her around to face him. Hot hungry eyes stared back at her. "You're a cruel woman, Caroline Portman." He took her hand and dragged her from the kitchen and away from temptation. "Let's get going."

Nine

Sam pulled up to the home snuggled up against Clear Lake, about fifty miles outside of Hope Wells. It had been a long drive and after today's excursion to Midland, he wondered if Caroline would mind. But she hadn't complained or asked too many questions. She'd just sat there next to him in his truck, making light conversation, looking more beautiful than a woman had a right to look.

He smiled at her sleeping form, her head resting sweetly against the windowpane. She'd dozed off about ten minutes ago. He watched her a moment until she sensed that they had stopped. She lifted up and fidgeted with her dress and hair, then gazed out the window.

"We're here," he said quietly.

"Here?" Caroline shot him a puzzled look. She glanced again at the house. "It's magnificent."

And it was. The lakeside manor had been built in the early days of the Triple B and the architectural design, along with the use of only premium materials, made this home one of their company's finest accomplishments. Sam had known the owners, now in their early seventies, for years. And when he'd placed a call to them yesterday, they'd offered up their home without question or qualm. They no longer lived here full-time and luckily for Sam, they were out of town for the entire month.

Sam exited the truck and opened the door for Caroline. She stepped out and, as if Cinderella was heading to the ball, she stood for a moment in awe. Then she turned to him. "I don't understand."

Lights shining from the perfectly groomed lawn illuminated her pretty puzzlement. Sam took her hand. "I did some work for the owners a while back. They let me use this place from time to time."

Caroline took a moment to let that sink in. Sam guided her to the side of the house. They entered through a tall decorative iron gate and proceeded toward the grounds in back. Moonlight shimmered on the lake and a boat dock appeared. Soft music seemed to drift by, out of nowhere. And then he led her toward the patio area where a round glass table dressed with linens and china appeared.

Dinner.

Sam had to commend the management company who worked for the Pattersons. They'd done everything according to his specifications. It'd been the only time since leaving Houston that Sam had used his name and position to get what he needed. The irony struck him. Here he'd spent most of his time convincing Caroline that he was a drifter, a loner with no ties and no roots, yet she was the one and *only* person for whom he'd been willing to compromise his rigid self-proclaimed rules.

Pulling rank to make the night special for Caroline was a no-brainer. But Sam hadn't enjoyed going back to his old ways to do it. The one-time CEO of a powerful company no longer thrived on getting what he wanted at any cost.

And Sam figured that was good thing.

"Sam," she said breathlessly, "this is…this is lovely. How did you—"

Sam kissed away her question. "Cinderella, enjoy the ball. Tomorrow we turn into pumpkins again."

Caroline chuckled, the warm rich sound of her laughter filling his head. And his heart. Sam fought the feeling. Fought the joy he felt just being with Caroline. He wanted to give her a special night, but he had to remind himself that this fairy tale would end differently. There would be no happily ever after. He had less than two weeks left at Belle Star before Annabelle returned. Sam had to be gone by then.

Sam led Caroline to the table and pulled out her chair. She tucked her bottom down and smiled her thank-you. "Hungry?" he asked.

"Famished."

Sam removed the lids that kept their meals warm and they gazed at a plate of scallops, shrimp and lobster baked in a lemon wine sauce over steaming hot angel-hair pasta. Bread and wine accompanied the meal.

"Not usual Texas fare. I hope you like it."

"It looks delicious, Sam, but I still don't know how you managed all this."

Sam smiled. "First dates should always leave an impression."

Caroline shook her head at him. "This one's going to be hard to beat."

That's what Sam secretly hoped. Though he would leave her one day soon, he wanted her to remember this night. He wanted her to know he felt her worthy of making an extra effort. She'd been through a bad marriage and she hadn't been treated right. If Sam could change that, he would. So he did the next best thing by showing her that she deserved nothing but the best.

They dug into the gourmet meal with gusto, each saying very little, but their eyes made contact often and the magnetic pull seemed to energize the warm air. When they were through, Sam rose and put out his hand. "Dance?"

"I'd love to."

And since the only music that had played all night had been slow sexy ballads, Sam took her into his arms, drawing her close. He breathed in her scent, memorizing the fragrance that he'd remember as Caroline's alone.

Sinful.

Caroline rested her head on his chest, their bodies pressed to one another's and they danced that way, with soft moonlight and music lulling them into the sort of peace that Sam had only known in her arms. And after three more ballads, Sam looked down into her eyes. "Want to see the lake?"

She nodded and together, hand-in-hand, they walked out onto the small wooden dock that jutted out into Clear Lake. They stood gazing at the water, the night air bringing a slight breeze. Sam wrapped his arm around her shoulder.

"Hmmm, it's so peaceful here." As Caroline gazed out, her blue eyes caught the light of the moon, the sparkle a sight to behold.

"It's quiet and secluded. A good place to think."

"Or not think."

"Right. Not thinking is good too," Sam said, meaning every word. He'd done his share of overthinking everything in his life and he'd just recently learned that not thinking was sometimes the better choice. "How'd you get so smart?"

Caroline chuckled. "Flattery will get you everywhere."

"Oh, yeah? What if where I want to go isn't appropriate on a first date?"

She looked into his eyes. God, she was so beautiful, so intelligent and so incredibly sexy. "You're doing great so far. I'd say, take your best shot."

He took her hand and led her off the dock. They walked along a darkened path where the moonlight touched the lake's surface, casting slight shades of light. Sam stopped amid a cluster of tall oak trees, leaning up against one, pulling Caroline in close. He lifted the hem of her dress, inching it up her legs. He stroked her thighs up and down, her soft creamy skin under his palms heating him instantly. Then he inched his fingers up and played with the lace of her panties. "I've wanted to do this all night," he whispered, kissing her lips roughly.

Caroline moaned.

He tugged her panties down and worked them off slowly, letting her step out of them. "And this." He cupped her between the thighs, spreading her legs, his palm open, skimming the soft folds there. She bucked and moved against his hand.

"Feels so good, Sam," she whispered urgently.

"Damn it, Caroline, I'm gonna die a happy man." Sam moved with her now, stroking her until he needed more. With his other hand, he lowered the top of her clingy red dress, exposing a tiny red-lace bra barely keeping her full breasts from exploding out. Sam maneuvered that undergarment off in seconds, and lowered his mouth to one globe, taking her into his mouth. She gasped and threw her head back, her blond hair tumbling out of its confinement. Sam moistened her with his tongue, making wide sweeping circles until the very tip of her breast pebbled hard and erect.

Caroline moaned again, softer now, more intensely. "That's it, sweetheart," he said and he felt the pressure building. She rode his hand now, bucking against him, and when he'd reached his limit he set her aside, unzipped his pants, taking out a condom quickly and then twirled her around. The wall of the oak braced her back and he impaled her with one swift efficient thrust.

Their groans met and lingered. Sam held her tightly

and allowed the initial mind-blowing union between their bodies to take hold. Caroline opened her eyes and met his gaze as he began to thrust into the sweetly familiar cove that welcomed him.

Sam lifted her then and she wrapped her legs around him. They moved as one until they succumbed to the heat, the force and the power developing between them. They climaxed together and gasped out their intoxicating release.

Caroline lowered her feet to the ground and they clung to each other. It was the best sex of his life, but it was more than that. And as Sam held her, he knew that he'd been a fool. A stupid, crazy fool—because how on earth could he believe that he could make love to this beautiful, gutsy, intelligent woman every night and not fall for her?

"Sam, I love it here," she said with a deep sigh, "but it's getting late. Shouldn't we get going?"

Grateful for the interruption of his thoughts, he answered, "Only if you want to, sweetheart."

"We have a long drive."

"We could stay here. The Pattersons wouldn't mind at all."

"Really? But I didn't bring anything with me."

Sam chuckled. "I managed to snag both of our toothbrushes before we left."

Caroline shook her head, looking at him with a twinkle in her eyes.

"They have five bedrooms here," he said.

"It is a *long* drive home, isn't it?" Caroline didn't

want the night to end any more than he did. "We'd have to be up and gone by the crack of dawn. Tomorrow's a work day."

They'd both agreed that if they'd played on Saturday, then they'd turn Sunday into a workday. And they had played. Sam loved playtime with Caroline. "If the boss lady says we work, then we work. So what do you say? Want to stay the night?"

Caroline smiled and nodded. "Well, since you went to the trouble of bringing our toothbrushes."

Sam picked up her bra and panties, stuffing them into his pocket. Caroline adjusted her dress, shifting it back into place as Sam looked on. Just knowing she wore that dress now without benefit of underwear shook him to the core. The material hung on every curve, every hollow and her pebble-hard nipples jutting out, defining the rounded shapes of her breasts and keeping the dress in place, worked on making a spent man hot and ready again. He took her hand. "Let's try out one of their bedrooms, darlin'."

Or with the way he'd begun to feel about Caroline, maybe they'd try out all five.

On Monday morning, Caroline sat down at her computer thanking high heaven for online banking. She'd saved a ton of work and many trips to town by setting up this new method of bill-paying.

She'd been on fire lately, eager to start advertising the grand opening of Belle Star in two weeks. She'd already contacted local newspapers and had flyers made up, along with commissioning a huge banner that she'd designed to welcome the visitors to her new stables. She planned a huge Texas-size barbecue with Maddie and several other friends offering to lend a hand. In her mind, it would be the perfect celebration to bring back old customers and garner some new ones as well.

When the phone rang, Caroline's heart sped up. She lifted the receiver and answered, taking her eyes off the computer screen to give her full attention to the caller.

"Hi, Mommy."

"Annabelle, sweetheart. Good morning. How's my favorite girl?"

"'Kay. Grammy said I could call 'cause to tell you good morning. We're going to Anna Marie's birthday party today."

"Oh, that's so nice, sweetie. I know you'll have fun at Anna Marie's today. How old will she be?" Caroline asked, knowing that her mother's friend's grandchild was just a baby.

"She's gonna be one, Mommy. I get to change her diaper at the party."

"That's my big girl."

"And we get rainbow cake and pony rides."

"Mmm. Cake sounds yummy. You be careful on the pony. Remember what Mommy always says?"

She could sense her daughter nodding into the phone.

"What does Mommy say?" Caroline asked again.

"Mommy says hold tight and re-spect the pony."

"That's right. And what does *respect* mean?"

"Means to be nice, right Mommy?"

Caroline laughed. "That's right, sweetheart. You did remember, you smart girl."

Annabelle giggled, the sound sheer pleasure to Caroline's ears. She missed her daughter terribly. But keeping busy had helped ease some of her loneliness.

"I love you, sweetheart."

"Love you too, Mommy. Here's Grammy. She wants to talk."

"Okay, have fun at the party."

Caroline finished her conversation with her mother and hung up the phone. She always needed a minute after one of Annabelle's phone calls to reassemble her thoughts. She couldn't wait to hold her daughter in her arms again. And tuck her into bed. She even missed waking up in the middle of the night just to check on her, to make sure she was sleeping peacefully.

Lord, motherhood was wonderful. And trying. And blessed. And every other emotion she could imagine wrapped into one tight, almost-five-year-old bundle.

"Coffee's ready," Sam called out from the kitchen.

Caroline smiled. She'd gotten used to having Sam here. Still on a high from their first "date," Caroline had daydreamed all of yesterday, barely able to keep up with Sam's relentless quest to finish painting the second stable. They'd worked their fingers to the bone and then fallen into bed exhausted last night.

Caroline couldn't have asked for a better worker. Sam did the work of two men, never stopping until he was satisfied. And at night, the same held true, except he managed to satisfy them both. "I'll be right there."

Caroline checked her bank statement, ready to click off the computer, when something odd struck her. Neither of the checks she'd given to Sam for his weekly salary had been cashed.

She thought back on the lavish dinner and beautiful surroundings he'd supplied for their Saturday night date. She figured he'd used some of his earnings. So she couldn't imagine why Sam hadn't bothered to cash his checks. After all, he was a drifter with no roots and no great source of income. Or was he?

Caroline wandered into the kitchen ready to ask Sam about the uncashed checks. "Sam, I have a question."

But Sam wasn't in the kitchen. She found him standing on the back porch, looking skyward. Caroline followed the direction of his gaze, watching a helicopter hovering overhead, the flapping sounds becoming louder and louder as it zeroed in.

To her surprise, the helicopter set down on her property. Caroline bounded out the back door and shouted to compete with the roar of the powerful machine. "Sam, did you see that?"

Sam winced, then ran a hand down his jaw, but no surprise registered. He remained calm and nodded.

"Sam!"

"It's okay, Caroline," he shouted, then guided her back into the kitchen away from the deafening noise. He shut the back door and sighed with resignation. "I know who it is."

Angered and confused, Caroline's voice held no patience. "Well, *who's* landing a helicopter on my property for heaven's sake?"

Sam looked up at her like a child who'd been caught with both hands in the cookie jar. "My brother."

Caroline had a bad feeling about this. She stood just outside her back door with arms folded, waiting for Sam to return. He'd said to wait until he found out what was going on, and then he'd explain everything to her. Now, she watched him out in the south end of the property speaking adamantly with his brother. The two had been out there for quite some time. And from what she could see of the helicopter, it sported some sort of fancy emblem on the side, though she couldn't make out what it said.

Sam had a lot of explaining to do and she figured that she wouldn't like any of it.

Finally, the two men approached and Caroline immediately saw the resemblance. Sam's brother was younger, perhaps a little more lean, but those dark eyes and that crop of dark hair couldn't be missed. Both men wore a somber expression. When they finally reached her back porch, Sam spoke up. "Caroline Portman, I'd like you to meet my brother, Wade. Wade, this is Caroline."

Wade put out his hand. "Sorry about landing the chopper here. I had to find Sam immediately. There's been some bad news."

Caroline took Wade's hand in a brief handshake. She still didn't know what any of this meant. And the resemblance at close range was remarkable. Both men were gorgeous. "What kind of bad news?"

Wade stepped back. "I'll let Sam explain."

Sam shot him an impatient glare.

"Your stuff is in the tack room at the back of the stables, right?" Wade asked.

Sam closed his eyes for a second. "Most of it, yeah."

Wade smiled at Caroline. "It's a pleasure, ma'am. I'll let you two talk now."

Both of them watched Wade's back as he headed for the stables. "What's this all about?" Caroline asked with a sense of impending doom.

Sam took a deep breath, his chest heaving. "Let's go inside. Have that cup of coffee. There's a lot to tell."

Caroline's legs went weak from his tone, and only with Sam's guidance, a hand to her back, did she muster the steps necessary to go inside. There, she sat while Sam poured them both a fresh cup of coffee.

"I just found out that my father died last night. The heart attack took him quickly."

Caroline gasped. She hadn't expected this. "Oh, Sam. I'm so sorry."

Sam shook his head. "Don't waste your sympathy on him, Caroline. I'll explain about my father later, but first you have to know that I never meant to hurt anyone, especially not you."

Caroline's eyes rounded, her heart beating fast. "What will hurt me?"

"I'm hoping nothing, but then I'm a bit of a fool when it comes to you, darlin'. You see, my father owned and operated the biggest construction company in the Southwest, the Triple B, which stands for Blake Beaumont Building. And for the past nine years, I've been the CEO and my father's right-hand man. Well, up until eight months ago, that is."

"When you lost your daughter?"

Sam nodded. "Yes, about then. The long and the short of it is that I hated the man I'd become. I couldn't live with myself and I hated everything about my father's company. So I took off. I left the Triple B and my father, leaving behind my old way of life. I needed to do that for my sanity, Caroline. I couldn't live with myself another minute.

"As a young boy all I wanted was my father's love. I'd tried everything I could to be worthy in his eyes until I finally understood what I needed to do. The Triple B meant everything to him, so if I could make him an even bigger success, if I could earn his respect, I thought I'd also earn his love. But I realized far too late, that my father wasn't capable of loving anyone or anything but the Triple B. And I'd allowed him to suck me into his web quite easily.

"I'm a millionaire, Caroline. I have more money than any one person could ever need or want. But the price of my success was far too high. I was the worst kind of husband and father. I neglected everyone in favor of the company. In the end, I sacrificed my daughter's life. And now, it seems that I'm heir to my father's legacy."

Caroline listened, her heart breaking for Sam's loss, but her head spinning in anger and betrayal. Sam was a millionaire, doing what? Playing at being a lonely drifter with no money and no roots? He'd been deceitful and Caroline couldn't get past his duplicity.

"So, you decided lying to me was your best bet? You'd simply string the young widow along, giving me your one-month deadline. How many other women have you done this to? How many others have you lied to? I'm sorry for what you've gone through, Sam. Lord knows, I'd be a heartless mother not to recognize your grief, but you had no right to do this to me. You lied to me. You betrayed me."

"No, Caroline. I never betrayed you."

"I don't know you, Sam."

"You *do* know me. You can trust me."

Caroline didn't trust anyone at the moment. She glanced out the window, her nerves raw, her heart aching. "Your brother has packed your stuff up. He's waiting for you by the helicopter." Caroline realized that Sam would leave now, days before he'd intended. And all those old feelings of abandonment when Gil left came rushing back. The haunting memory of his betrayal was fresh again. She trembled, fighting off those old feelings of failure and turned away from Sam. "Go back to wherever you're really from, Sam."

"Houston. But it's not my home anymore, Caroline. That's what I'm trying to tell you. I never meant for any of this to touch you." He came to stand in front of her, so that she had to look into his eyes—eyes that had lied to her one too many times.

"Well, it has, hasn't it?"

"I'm sorry. Truly sorry. But I'm not Gil. I won't abandon you. And hell, Caroline, I've never felt this way about another woman. That's not what this was about. I never stayed in one place long enough to get involved with anyone. I didn't want to get involved with you, as you might remember."

"Oh, so now it's my fault? I was the desperate, needy woman who threw herself at you?" With arms folded, Caroline's face flamed. She recognized the truth in that, which made her even angrier.

Sam bit his lip. He shook his head. He let a beat pass, then another, as if he had to rein in his own anger. "No, you were the gorgeous, courageous woman I couldn't keep my hands off, if you want the truth. And I did get involved. Too involved. I don't know where it's going with us, but I do know that I'll be back to help you finish Belle Star, Caroline. But right now, I have to leave. I don't want to, but Wade needs me. He's a bit out of his element right now. There are papers to sign and a whole lot of red tape. I'll make it quick. I'll be back as soon as I can."

"That's what I thought when Gil left. That he'd come back."

Sam took her into his arms. She allowed him to, because she didn't have the strength to fight him. He pressed his face close to hers, making her look into his eyes. "I'm not Gil. Just give me a few days."

"That's up to you, Sam."

"So, you won't throw me out when I return?"

She shook her head. "No. We had a deal."

"Right, and I'll honor my part of the deal. I promise."

Wade started up the helicopter engine and from the corner of her eye she saw the blades beginning their rotation. "You'd better go."

Sam stared at her lips. Caroline pulled away.

"I'll be back," he said before walking out the door and if she hadn't been so heartbroken, she might have laughed at the cliché.

Ten

"It's not the end of the world that Sam's a millionaire with good looks to spare, my friend," Maddie said, pulling up a thick weed along the shady side of the house. Both women wore heavy gloves and were armed with small hand shovels. "I agree that he should have been honest with you."

Caroline yanked hard, pulling up a stubborn dead bush, the hard work easing her frustration. "He lost his daughter and blames himself, that much I get. But why lie to me? Why couldn't he tell me the truth? I would have understood."

Maddie stopped tugging long enough to meet Caroline's gaze. "Maybe because he could barely face the truth himself. Drifting from place to place, keeping his distance from everyone—maybe that was his way of coping with his loss. Maybe running was his only salvation."

Caroline shook her head. "He didn't have to lie to me. He knew about Gil and what I went through with him. I'd been open and honest, foolish me."

Maddie found a wilted plant from last year's garden and began to dig. "You're right. He's a creep. A scoundrel. Maybe you should toss him off the property when he comes back."

"*If* he comes back. I'm not holding my breath. And he's not a creep. A scoundrel maybe," Caroline said softly.

"For taking your heart?"

Caroline tossed the weeds in the garbage can she'd pulled up to the wall and began turning over the soil with her shovel. "There is that. I may have fallen for him, but I don't trust him. How could I? I thought I knew him."

"Maybe you do know him. Ever think about that? Maybe he's through being his father's man now. Maybe the Sam Beaumont you've come to know is really the man that he is."

Caroline thought she'd be a fool to hope. She'd learned hard lessons from Gil. She wouldn't give an inch this time. *This time,* she knew better. She dug deeper into the soil, lifting and tossing the dirt, making a nice bed for the hibiscus and gardenia bushes she planned to plant there.

"He's rich and the CEO of a giant construction company. Up until a few days ago I didn't know he'd been married or had a child. No, I don't really know Sam. None of this matters though, Maddie. He's got responsibilities in Houston now."

And what Caroline didn't add, but felt in her heart, was that Sam couldn't face seeing Annabelle. Thinking back now, he'd avoided all talk of her whenever possible. Caroline could only imagine his anguish at losing his daughter and ultimately feeling he'd caused her death. How hard it must have been for him to see Annabelle's things about. And now she understood why he'd avoided looking at the photos in her room—Annabelle's sunny face smiling into the camera was too hard to bear.

Caroline ached for Sam.

But she still felt betrayed.

"It's been three days," Maddie said. "Have you heard from him?"

"He's called every day and leaves a message."

"Because you won't pick up the phone?"

"Busted on that. I wouldn't know what to say to him. Besides, he only asks about Belle Star. How is the work going? How am I doing? He doesn't say anything about returning here."

"Sounds like the man cares about you."

Caroline shrugged and patted the soil down with her gloved hands. "If he comes back, it'll be all business. My personal time with Sam is over."

She almost said that she'd had her little fling, but it hadn't been that way with Sam. For her, it had been something special, so she wouldn't trivialize it. The memories wouldn't fade anytime soon. She knew that for certain.

She still loved him.

The scoundrel.

After lunch, Caroline bid farewell to Maddie, thanking her for the help. She finished up planting in the afternoon and worked into the evening on odds and ends. Tomorrow she'd try her hand working inside the stables.

She fell into bed just before ten o'clock, exhausted.

The next morning Caroline woke up feeling refreshed from a good night's sleep. She rose quickly, dressed in her work clothes, jeans and an old tank top that read Rhinestone Cowgirl with half of the pink sequins missing. The summer had heated up, and now gray clouds hovered overhead, causing the humidity in the air to rise considerably.

Caroline headed to the kitchen and brewed coffee. While she waited for the coffeemaker to fill the pot the sound of banging coming from the stables caught her attention. She listened carefully, and, no, she hadn't been mistaken. The hammering sound grew louder when she opened the back door.

Caroline poured herself a cup of coffee and strode purposely toward the sound. When she entered the stables she found herself face to face with Sam Beaumont. Bare-chested, wearing jeans and a studious expression, he was hammering a replacement plank onto one of the stalls.

Her heart in her throat, she remained speechless watching Sam's efficient movements as he continued to work.

"You still mad at me?" he asked, taking a moment to meet her eyes.

Her joy at seeing him, at his return, warred with the

sense of betrayal and disappointment she felt. But no, she no longer held on to her anger. How could she be angry with a man who'd looked bone-tired and weary, as though he hadn't gotten a wink of sleep, while he worked on her stables?

He'd come back, just like he said he would. But things had to be different between them now. She had to protect what was left of her heart.

"I have one question and I'd like an honest answer. The night we went...the night you took me to Clear Lake."

He nodded. "I remember."

As if either of them could forget that wonderful night.

"Do you own that house?"

Sam looked up from his stall, removing his heavy work gloves to look squarely into her eyes. "No. I don't own that house, Caroline, but I built it."

"Oh," Caroline muttered, "no wonder you knew your way around so well."

"I didn't lie to you about that."

"Didn't you?" She kept the accusation out of her tone, but felt it deep inside. There was so much to Sam Beaumont that she didn't know. So many facets to his life he hadn't wanted to share. And now, it seemed too late.

"I told you I'd done some work for the owners."

"It's a beautiful house," she said, lost in thoughts of his craftmanship and work ethic. She couldn't begrudge him that. But he had lied to her, over and over again, and he might think his explanation good enough, but Caroline, a woman who'd had the rug pulled out from under her one too many times, Caroline recognized that truth.

"It was one of the first ones we'd built together, my father and I. My design, his corrections." Sam smiled wistfully. "It had been my pride and joy, until…" He stopped and shrugged, and Caroline sensed that he'd been thinking of his daughter.

"I didn't think you'd come back."

"I would have been here sooner, but the funeral was yesterday and I couldn't get out of going. Family and friends expected me there."

"You look tired."

Sam inhaled sharply. "Haven't gotten much sleep lately."

Caroline handed him her mug of coffee. She hadn't yet touched a drop. "Here. Take a break."

The irony in what she'd just said struck Caroline with clarifying force. Offering Sam Beaumont, the CEO and heir to a multi-million-dollar company, a cup of coffee and allowing him break time seemed so odd.

Sam took the cup, his fingers brushing slightly over hers. The contact hit a nerve with her, and she backed away. She couldn't weaken. She had to keep to her resolve. Sam would leave sooner rather than later, and protecting herself would be crucial to her survival.

Sam leaned against the stall post and sipped his coffee, closing his eyes as if relishing the taste. "I missed…your coffee."

Caroline didn't respond. Lord, how she'd missed him.

"Looks like you've gotten some work done in here," he said, glancing around, seeing firsthand what had already been accomplished.

"Jack came by the other day. He spent his day off from the jail working with me."

Sam stopped the coffee mug, just before reaching his lips. "Jack, huh?"

"He got a lot done that day." She felt she had to defend Jack's efforts. "He never let up. He's been a good friend."

Sam listened, sipping his coffee, and nodded.

"Sam, I can't say I'm not surprised that you came back. Judging from the work you're used to doing, this must seem trivial to—"

"Not trivial, darlin'. If it's important to you, how can it be? It's your livelihood and your legacy to your daughter. No, I don't look at it as trivial at all."

"Thank you." She felt as though he really meant that. "But what I was about to say, is that things have changed between us now. If you want to stay and see this through with me, I would appreciate it. But you and I…well, it's over."

Sam pursed his lips and looked away for a moment. Then he met her eyes with softness and understanding. "I figured as much."

"And you still came back?"

"A deal's a deal. Besides, I've got something invested in this place, too. I want to see your success."

Caroline smiled for the first time in four days. Then she remembered that Sam would leave soon. She couldn't allow the warm tingling feelings surging up her body. She had to hang on to some of her misgivings. "Don't say nice things to me, Sam. Let's keep it all business."

Sam chuckled as if what she'd said had been ridiculous. "Don't know if I can do that, Caroline."

"You have to, Sam," she said vehemently.

"Why?" He looked genuinely puzzled as if he hadn't a clue.

"Because I really need your help."

"I know that, sweetheart. That's why I came back."

"And because…" she began but couldn't go on.

"Because?" he asked softly, his brows furrowed, his eyes probing.

"Because, I've fallen in love with you, you idiot!"

Sam braced himself against the stall, watching Caroline storm out of the building, her parting words a shock to his system.

Caroline loved him.

He hadn't expected it. Nor had he expected to be encased in the soft afterglow of those words. It surrounded him with warmth and goodness and everything Sam didn't deserve. Yet, the glow stayed, like energy circling his body, those sweet words reverberating in his ears.

I've fallen in love with you, you idiot!

For a moment Sam smiled, thinking he'd heard better declarations, but the smile faded soon enough.

And so did the afterglow. Sam felt cold inside now, a frigid wave passing over him. He hadn't wanted this. He hadn't wanted to hurt Caroline Portman. There was no hope for the two of them. There never had been.

Maybe if he'd told her the truth from the beginning, she might have realized she shouldn't have wasted time on a man who'd never win a husband-of-the-year award. He'd never be able to face little Annabelle, either. He should have told her everything up front and maybe they wouldn't have gotten so deeply involved.

But God, it was good to see her again. He'd missed her. Missed everything about her. And just seeing her walk into the stables, offering him a cup of coffee, her blond hair flowing and that tight faded tank top clinging to her body, had nearly sent him to his knees. She was the most beautiful, courageous woman he'd ever met. And he didn't deserve her.

He'd had to think twice about coming back, wondering if a clean break would have been easier. But Sam couldn't abandon her, not when she needed him. He'd given his word and that much about him *had* changed. He would rather have cut off his right arm than not return to finish what he'd started. He could do that much for Caroline. He could get the stables ready for her grand opening.

Sam took half a second debating what to do. He had to speak with Caroline, though he didn't know what he could say to make things better for her. Nothing had changed. He still had to leave when the work was done. But damn it, he had to try.

He strode into the yard and made it to the back door within seconds. The screen door slapped from behind when he entered, startling Caroline from her spot by the kitchen sink. She looked up and didn't give him a chance to speak.

"Don't say anything, Sam. Not one word. I said what

I said, and I meant it, but I would take those words back in a minute if I could. You're not obligated to me in any way. Go back and finish what you were doing. I'll call you when lunch is ready."

Caroline turned her back on him and continued rinsing out the coffeepot.

The tic in Sam's jaw worked overtime. He stood there gazing at her with both anger and pride. The woman always seemed to elicit conflicting emotions within him. Today was no exception. But damn, he couldn't just walk out of here and not have his say. She needed to hear some things, whether she wanted to or not.

Sam took the steps necessary to stand behind her. Both arms reached around to brace the kitchen counter, trapping her from moving.

"Caroline, I have some things to say to you. Some of them are *nice* and some are gonna be damn hard to hear, so just stand still and listen."

Sam stood close enough to breathe in her scent, a heady mix of soap and flowers and Caroline. In a weaker moment, he would have wrapped her into his arms by now, but that wouldn't happen today or any other day. She'd made her feelings clear. And Sam would respect that.

He spoke from behind, holding her to the spot. "Are you willing to listen?"

"Do I have a choice?"

"No."

Her stance relaxed then and Sam realized she'd been rigid and nervous before. "I'm listening."

"None of this was what I expected, Caroline. I never would have taken the job if it meant hurting you in the process. I've been drifting from town to town for months, trying to piece my life back together. Yes, I've been running away, but it's all I know to do. Up until I came here, I didn't know a peaceful night's sleep. I had hard times facing the days, but nights were the worst.

"Where others say I will heal in time, I don't think it's possible. The pain inside me goes deep. It's raw and gnaws at me every day. I was a worthless husband and a terrible father. I neglected everyone I cared about. And what's really pathetic is that I didn't even recognize what I had until it was too late.

"You're a beautiful woman, Caroline, inside and out. I admire everything you're doing here. You've had some rough times in your life as well, but you didn't give up. You've got a good plan and you won't let anything get in your way.

"Walking away from you is going to be harder on me than you might think. I didn't mean to, but I got involved. Deeply involved. And honey, I just can't afford that. I'm still running. Can you understand that?"

Caroline nodded and when Sam released his arms to come around to look at her, silent tears were rolling down her cheeks. The ache in the pit of his stomach intensified and only confirmed what he'd always recognized. He was no good for Caroline. He'd hurt her and would only continue to bring her pain.

"Ah, sweetheart," he said, unable to keep from touching

her. He wound his hand around her neck and brought her close, wiping her tears with the back of his thumb.

Caroline stepped away. "You're being nice again," she said on a shaky breath.

Sam dropped his arms. "Sorry."

She cast him half a smile. "I get it, Sam. I always have. I can't help how I feel any more than you can. I know you have to go. I know it in my head at least."

Sam nodded, understanding that what's in the heart is a whole lot more potent and a whole lot more dangerous. "I came back here to help you achieve your dream. I know that's important to you. I'm willing to stay until we're finished, if you still want me here."

"I still want you here, Sam."

"Then I'm staying."

Caroline nodded then smiled. "Okay."

And as Sam walked to the back door, she added, "Annabelle is coming home on Sunday night."

Sam strode out the door, his gut twisting into a knot. He had three days to finish the work here because come Sunday morning he had to be gone.

Eleven

Saturday morning dawned with clouds and a gloomy sky. A light drizzle moistened the ground and Caroline could only thank heaven that the stables were all but finished. Early this morning she and Sam had cleaned out all remnants of the old straw and bedding in each stall. They had worked like demons sweeping out the stalls and inserted what Caroline deemed her only real luxury, stall mats. The mats that had been custom-sized, would protect the ground beneath and would reduce the amount of straw and shavings she'd need inside each.

They'd eaten lunch late and, as usual these days, their conversation bordered on quiet and cordial, each one feeling their own sense of grief. Caroline's anticipation over seeing Annabelle tomorrow night had been weighted only by the thought of never seeing Sam

Beaumont again. She told herself that her dream of Belle Star Stables was finally coming true and she should be rejoicing instead of feeling the hours tick by like a woman walking toward her own execution.

Caroline sat at the kitchen table now, staring at the brochures and price lists from her competition in the area. She needed to make money, but she also had to be practical. First and foremost, she needed to garner some business which required her to post the most competitive prices she possibly could. When she opened her doors next week at her grand opening, she'd have brochures of her own along with a list of services and fees.

"You ready for me?" Sam asked, whipping off his hat and stepping into the kitchen. He tossed his hat in Frisbee fashion onto the kitchen counter, a gesture Caroline had come to think as his alone.

"Not a minute too soon. I've been going over these, but I could sure use your input. Any problems on the grounds?"

Sam had taken Dumpling on one last tour of the grounds to scour the fences and pasture to make sure there wasn't anything they'd overlooked. "Everything looks good out there. We didn't miss anything." Sam sat down next to her. "What smells so darn good?"

"Cookies. Chocolate chip," Caroline said absent-mindedly. "Annabelle's favorites."

Sam nodded and glanced toward her range. It was just one more reminder that tomorrow their lives would change. For Caroline, hers would go back to normal, the way it had always been, but she wondered what life had in store for Sam.

"You sharing?"

She smiled. "I made a pan just for you."

"For me?"

She shoved the brochures his way. "It's a bribe. I need to figure out how to make this all work. And you're elected to help me."

Sam frowned. "You got milk to go with those cookies?"

She nodded.

"Okay, then let's get to work."

Sam studied the figures and her set-up costs, working up a fee list that would compete with other stables while giving her enough of a profit to stay in business. After half an hour, he said, "These fees will keep you afloat, but the real profit to be made is in any extras you can include, such as riding lessons and selling small items and riding gear. You need strict rules and must make sure everyone who boards a horse pays on time. Do you have anyone lined up to help you?"

"I've spoken with one high-school boy who'll be available in the early mornings and after school. And there's a young girl who recently dropped out of college who used to babysit Annabelle once in a while. She loves horses and is willing to work full-time for the time being. I think I'm covered."

Sam slid the fee schedule over to her. "Take a look and make changes if you want. But this is what I feel would work for you."

Caroline rose from her seat and slid the cookies she'd

baked onto a large plate. She brought the plate to the table, setting it in front of Sam. On impulse, she picked up one warm cookie oozing soft chocolate and lifted it to Sam's mouth. "I trust your instincts, Sam."

Sam took a bite of the cookie and when she made a move to pull away, he grabbed her wrist. The connection heated her skin. She lifted her eyes to his and saw a hunger that matched her own. She hadn't touched him since he'd come back, and now her foolish maneuver sizzled between them. She wanted his touch, his hands on her, their bodies pressed together, but at that very moment Sam released her hand.

She backed up a step. "I'll, uh, get the milk." She turned to the refrigerator, ready to open the door.

"I don't want milk, Caroline."

Caroline spun around but was saved from Sam's heated stare. The phone rang.

She lifted the receiver immediately and when the brief phone call was over, she turned to Sam, overjoyed. "Sam, that was Lone Star. I was approved! I'm going to adopt Princess!"

Sam rose from his seat and opened his arms. Without thought to propriety or her guarded uncertainties Caroline flew into his arms, unable to contain her delight. His embrace felt so right, so real and they remained that way, holding on to each other for a long moment. He pulled back long enough to look into her eyes. "I knew you'd get approved, sweetheart. You're perfect." He brought her close again and hugged tight. "Absolutely perfect."

"This is going to make Annabelle so happy," she said, then caught her mistake. Since finding out about Sam's loss, she'd tried to be sensitive to his feelings. Losing a child had to be devastating enough, but with Sam, the pain of his guilt went deeper than she might imagine. "Sam, I'm sorry. I shouldn't have said—"

"Shh, it's okay." He put a finger to her lips, keeping her from finishing her apology. "You're happy. And I'm happy for you. You deserve nothing but the best."

He moved his hand to her cheek, spreading his palm and cradling her. She turned her head into his hand, absorbing his tenderness. "Oh, Sam."

"Don't think I won't miss you, darlin'. I'll be gone but you'll be in my thoughts every day."

Caroline wrapped her arms around Sam's neck. She looked deeply into his eyes, and his gentle expression was too much to bear. With a desperate need to have this man hold her one last time throughout the night, she spoke from her heart. "We have tonight, Sam. Let's not waste it."

Sam closed his eyes and nodded and when he opened them again, she witnessed his desire warring with self-restraint.

"I'm sure, Sam. It's what I want and you said it yourself. I deserve the best."

Sam smiled. "In that case." He lifted her into his arms and headed for her bedroom.

Caroline lay curled up on the bed, the cotton sheet in a tangle around her body as she watched Sam lift up from the mattress to open the window and part the curtains. Soft rain fell and the air that rushed inside filled the room with crisp dewy freshness.

Sam peered out the window and she continued to watch the shadows play against his form, bared to her, strong and powerful. They'd made love once already and her memory would be forever painted with vivid, sexy images.

Caroline rose from the bed and walked over to him. She stood beside him and he wrapped his arm around her shoulder. They both stood there watching the sky above, listening to the sound of rain hitting the ground. Gray clouds covered the stars, but Caroline imagined them, twinkling above, ready to spread light rays when the clouds dispersed.

They'd spent the better part of the afternoon and night in bed, holding each other, making love and dozing in peaceful sleep. Caroline remembered what Sam had said about not knowing a good night's sleep until he'd come here. For that, she was grateful and she wondered how either of them would sleep once he was gone. Time ticked by too quickly—they had only a few fragile hours left.

"It's a magical night, Sam."

Sam turned to face her, his eyes a shadow of sadness. He put a finger to her cheek and outlined her jaw then caressed her lips, his touch oh so tender. He brought his lips down on hers, kissing her softly with the utmost care. "I love you, Caroline. I know that now. But I can't stay."

Caroline rejoiced for a moment, glad to have Sam's love. She hadn't thought him capable of ever loving again, and just the fact that he'd admitted his love for her meant certain progress. She should be overjoyed. But in her heart, she wasn't entirely sure if he knew the emotion fully. She believed he loved her, but not enough to overcome his own fears and misgivings—and certainly not enough to conquer his guilt. The brutal reality never veered far from her thoughts. She knew Sam had to leave. She'd always known.

"It's okay, Sam," she said for his benefit. Inside, her heart tore in two.

"I want nothing but the best for you, sweetheart. Your stables will be a succ—"

"Shh," she said, stopping him from finishing his thoughts. She didn't want his admiration or his encouragement. Not tonight. Tonight, she only wanted his love. "Let's go back to bed, Sam."

He stared into her eyes, and nodded with understanding. He took her hand, leading her back to bed. She lay down and reached up for him. He came down on top of her, their bodies pressed to one another. "Make love to me, Sam. Once more."

They both knew it would be their last time together.

Sam cradled her in his arms and skimmed his lips over every inch of her, making her heart soar and her body hum. His touch created sensations that both aroused her and made her feel like a precious treasure. He kissed her gently, caressed her skin, rounding her breasts with his palms then sweeping his hands down lower until she became lost to everyone and everything but the heady, loving stirrings Sam created.

She melted into him and he into her. They moved as one, with cravings and yearnings that tore at her soul. She kissed him fervently, caressed his chest, skimmed his navel and lower yet, to feel his powerful erection in her hand. She stroked him soundly, memorizing the feel of him, his silky strength. She tasted him and he groaned, stroking her with his hands spread, their bodies entwined.

And when he nudged the tip of her womanhood, she ached for him. He entered her then, and she welcomed him, the movements new and familiar all at the same time.

He lifted up and gazed into her eyes. She met his eyes and they moved together with thrusts that peaked, tearing a gut-wrenching cry from her throat. He filled her and she took every last ounce he offered, until they reached as high as two souls could possibly go.

They shattered at the same time, both crying out each other's names with declarations of love and bittersweet longing.

And when their breaths steadied and their bodies relaxed, Caroline felt safe and secure in Sam's arms once again.

For the very last time.

Caroline woke to a murky day, the tumultuous clouds outside no match for her own sense of gloom. She reached out to touch the empty space beside her in the bed and knew that Sam had left her in the wee hours of the morning. She rose slowly, fighting off her tears, shoring up her courage and thinking of making it through one day at a time.

She showered and dressed in her usual work clothes although she didn't have too much work left to do. Amazingly, she and Sam had made a great team. They'd gotten everything done she'd hoped to and now the stables were ready for honest-to-goodness-paying customers.

The only bright spot in this dismal day was that Annabelle would return home. Caroline's parents would travel with her and they'd stay for a few days before heading back to Florida. Caroline had wanted them to stay for her grand opening, but her father's health wasn't what it had once been. It was enough that they would see Belle Star Stables the way she'd always envisioned it. Her dream of refurbishing the stables had come true.

Caroline entered the kitchen and set the coffeepot to brewing. A cloud of loneliness surrounded her. She would drink coffee alone this morning. There would be no more sharing of thoughts and dreams with Sam. There would be no more late-night dinners. There would be no more cuddling in his arms and lovemaking until dawn.

Caroline sat at the kitchen table, her head in her hands. When the front doorbell rang, she couldn't help but hope that Sam had returned, but as she glanced out the parlor window on her way to reach the door, those hopes all but shattered. A rain-splattered patrol car from the Hope Wells Sheriff's Department sat in her driveway,

She plastered on a big smile and opened the door. "Morning, Jack."

"Hey there," he said, entering without invitation. That's how it had always been with Jack. They'd been friends forever. He handed her a white bag. "I brought you doughnuts. Hey, cops don't have an exclusive on them, you know."

"So you've said about a…" she glanced into the bag loaded with maple, sugar, chocolate and lemon-filled doughnuts "…a *dozen* times. A dozen, Jack? Trying to fatten me up?"

"I thought you might need some nourishment."

She raised her eyebrows.

"Okay, I saw Sam driving out of town this morning. Thought you could use a friend."

"You're on a mission of mercy?"

He shrugged, then made his way into the kitchen. "Coffee ready?"

"Just about. Sit down. You're gonna help me eat some of these and the rest are going straight back to the sheriff's office. A girl's got to watch her figure, you know."

Jack sat down and dived into the bag, coming up with a maple bar. Before sliding it into his mouth, he took a slow leisurely tour of her body. If it were anyone else, she might have blushed. "You've got nothing to worry about." He winked. "Everything's in the right place."

She slumped into the chair and grabbed a chocolate doughnut. "Thanks."

"Really. All joking aside, how are you?"

Caroline set the doughnut down. "Annabelle's coming home today. Belle Star has never looked better. I'm good, Jack."

"You never were much good at lying." He took a giant bite of his doughnut and chewed thoughtfully. "Being honest to a fault has its drawbacks. Your friends can see right through you. And I don't like what I'm seeing."

"I'm afraid to ask."

"You fell for the guy. He lied to you and broke your heart."

"That's not true," she said, rushing to Sam's defense. "He didn't lie to me about leaving. He never gave me false hope."

"Ah, okay. So, you're...good."

"Yeah, I'm good."

Jack rose to lift the coffeepot from its cradle. He took two mugs out of the cabinet and poured, looking outside at the rain. "Hey, what's that?"

Caroline took another bite of her doughnut. "What's what?"

"Outside, on the back porch. Come take a look."

Caroline walked over the kitchen door and unlatched the lock, then opened the screen. A cool mist of rain surged forth as she stepped outside.

There, on the porch, shining with new red paint and rust-free straightened-out handlebars, sat Annabelle's tricycle—the one Caroline was sure had been ready for the garbage heap. Only Annabelle's pleas to keep the old thing had kept it from its true fate.

Her hands flew to her mouth. She gasped the moment realization dawned. "Sam."

And then tears she'd bravely held back all morning, flowed down her cheeks, rivaling the droplets pouring down from the darkened sky. Caroline knew what it must have cost Sam to fix Annabelle's dilapidated

tricycle. The memories it must have stirred up, the heartache he must have felt. She understood his pain and how
hard it was for him even to think of Annabelle without
reliving his own loss. For Caroline, what he'd done was
more than a kind gesture. It was an act of love.

Jack sidled up next to her and put his arms around
her shoulders, bringing her close. "Maybe he's not such
a jerk after all," he whispered into her ear.

She shook her head. Softly, she replied, "No, he's not
a jerk." Then she turned into Jack's embrace and sobbed
silently, the pain a physical ache to her heart.

"I'm such a damn jerk," Sam said, shoving aside a
stack of papers on his desk. He glanced at the clock on
the wall. He'd been at it all night—reviewing the
ongoing projects at the Triple B, dealing with his
father's attorneys and their requests, speaking with dis-
traught friends and family members.

Old familiar pangs of what life had been like just a
year ago plagued him. He'd worked through the dinner
hour and now it was nearly midnight. Fool that he was,
he hadn't stopped, but had kept up the pace, hating the
obligation, but assuming it nonetheless.

His eyes stung, his head ached. The knot in the pit
of his stomach burned deep. He hadn't eaten or slept
well in three days.

He hated sitting at his desk.

At one time, being set up in the father's old corner
office had meant everything to him. He'd come in that
first day on the job, taken his seat on the finest brown-

leather chair money could buy and swiveled it around, looking out the wall-to-wall glass window to view the magnificent Houston skyline and thought that he'd finally made it.

Now, he resented every piece of furniture, every honor and award displayed on the walls, every bit of opulence that at one time, had defined his success.

Too late, he'd learned the true meaning of success.

Caroline Portman had had a hand in that learning process, but he couldn't even begin to think about her. He hadn't, not consciously. He couldn't think about the amazing woman he'd left behind. But she stayed with him, buried deep, and unlike the other burdens he'd managed to stow away, she remained a vital part of him, unconsciously.

Sam stared down at the papers he had yet to review and cursed his fate. The life he'd run away from had come back to haunt him.

Wade strode into the office, his nose in a file. "We've got a problem with the Overton project."

Sam looked up. "What?"

Wade tossed the file on his desk. "Over budget, under-staffed. The folks in the community are kicking up a fuss. They're protesting at the site. Seems our fine citizens don't want the bar and grill going up."

"Why, is the food that bad?"

Wade chuckled. "What food? It's going to be a Coyote Ugly with dance poles."

Sam shoved the file aside. None of this mattered to him. He didn't want to be here. He didn't want any of the obligations that came with being Blake Beaumont's heir. He rubbed his eyes and yawned.

"Hey, when did you eat last?" Wade asked.

Sam shrugged. "Lunch, I think."

"Are you sleeping at all?"

Sam shrugged again. "Some."

"Liar. Go home, Sam. You look like crap."

"Thanks. Compliments will get you everywhere."

"I'm not joking. You look like you've been run over by a truck."

Sam glared at his brother.

Wade spread his arms out wide. "All of this can wait. The company isn't going to fall apart in a few days. Go home. Get some rest. We'll catch up on this stuff tomorrow. Better yet, I'll take you home and stay over at your place tonight."

"I don't need a babysitter, Wade."

"That's debatable. Come on, let's go." Wade gave him no option. He strode to the door and shut down the lights.

Later that night when Sam put his head to the pillow, he was glad that Wade had insisted on coming home with him. He'd missed his younger brother and the two had sat up for an hour, shooting the breeze, tossing back a few beers and reestablishing their relationship.

Sam closed his eyes and knew a minute of peace before images popped into his head. He thought of his daughter, Tess, her guileless innocence and the love she'd bestowed upon him even though he hadn't done anything much to earn that honor. Sam stored her sweet face away in his mind, holding on to the nuances that made her unique, and, only when he thought he could handle it did he upload those images to view and savor for a few precious moments.

Then his mind drifted to Caroline.

And a shallow gaping hole filled his heart. It seemed that Sam was destined to hurt the people he cared most about. But he could take some comfort that she should be happy now, having Annabelle home with her. He wondered if they'd picked up the filly, Princess, yet and could only imagine Caroline's joy at seeing her daughter's surprised face when she presented the pony to her.

After long restless minutes Sam finally slept, though fitfully, throughout the night.

The next day was more of the same. He sat in his large luxurious office, shuffling papers, trying to find a way to continue here. In truth, he hated the job, the company and everything that went along with it. No amount of money or accomplishment would change that.

But he stayed for Wade's sake. His younger brother had taken on the brunt of the work and the majority of their father's wrath when Sam had dropped the ball and taken off. He'd basically left Wade to hold down the fort. And Wade had worked doubly hard, never once complaining to Sam on those occasional phone calls they'd made to each other. No, Wade had been his sole source of emotional support. He'd let Sam go, had even encouraged it so that he could get a grip on his life.

Sam owed Wade.

He turned away from the desk and stared out the window. As much as he tried not to think of the woman he'd left behind, thoughts of Caroline entered his mind. He missed her terribly. He missed Belle Star and small-town life. He missed the simple things, like sharing a cup of coffee. Worrying over the price of feed and bedding. He even missed working long hours on the stables and the great sense of accomplishment that ensued once a project was finished.

But mostly, he missed Caroline's pretty blue eyes smiling at him.

"Go back to her."

Sam swiveled the chair around. Wade stood with his hands on his hips, shaking his head.

"What?"

"You're miserable here. Go back to Hope Wells. I figure Caroline wouldn't mind one bit."

Sam shook his head. "But I'd mind. I couldn't do that to her. I have the worst track record when it comes to marriage. And don't forget, she's got a daughter. It's a big responsibility. I don't think I'm capable, Wade. There have been too many failures in my life. Besides, I have a company to run. We've got ongoing projects and I can't ask you to do this all alone. You've already covered my butt countless times, as it is."

Wade braced both hands on Sam's desk and bent to look him in the eyes. "That's just it, Sam. Don't you get it? *You* are the heir to the Triple B. *You* can determine what happens to the company. *You* can sell it off. Break it up. Downsize. Hell, you can move a portion of it to, say, Hope Wells. The options are all yours. It's *your* company now."

Sam's eyes rounded in surprise. The company had

been a staple in the Beaumont family for years. He'd never thought of the possibility of selling, or moving or downsizing. It was obvious that Wade had been thinking with a clear mind, while Sam's head and heart had been muddled with confusion and doubt. "And what of you, little brother? It's your livelihood, too."

"Hell, we both have more money than we need now. I'm thinking that California sounds real good—the ocean breezes and all that. I could use a change of pace."

The phone in the outside office rang and Wade gestured for Sam to stay put. "Let me get it. Probably more complaints about the Overton project. I'll handle it. You sit back and think about what I just said."

Wade returned a minute later with a somber look. "Sam, that was one of Caroline's friends. There's been trouble at Belle Star."

Sam looked up. "What kind of trouble?"

"They've been having T-storms for days now. The land is flooded. And well, late last night, lightning struck down one of the trees on the property. It caught fire and spread to one of the stables. Seems there's a lot of destruction."

Sam rose to his feet. "Damn it."

"Wait, there's more. It seems that Caroline rushed into the stables to rescue her mare."

Sam's gut clenched. Dread and despair gripped him hard. "Don't tell me she's—"

"She's okay. She saved the mare and herself. But she's down with smoke inhalation."

Sam squeezed his eyes shut and cursed up a blue streak. "She's really okay, right?"

"Her friend said she should be fine in a few days."

"Was it Maddie?"

"No, some guy named Jack Walker."

Sam glared at his brother. "Did he say anything else?"

Wade scratched his head. "Yeah, uh, he did. He said that you shouldn't *screw* this up. And, bro, he didn't exactly use that word."

Sam nodded. He paced. He ran his hands through his hair. Frustrated and alarmed, he spoke quietly. "I wasn't there for her. I should have been there. She shouldn't have risked her life. Damn it."

"It's not your fault, Sam."

"Don't you see? I failed another person I care about. Caroline could have lost her life!"

"And *that* wouldn't have been your fault, either. But she's fine and you know what? I see this as a second chance for both of you. You might not have been there this time, but you can be there the next time. And the time after that. You can always be there for her. If you love this woman, you deserve to give it a chance."

There was no doubt in Sam's mind that he loved Caroline. Just thinking of her rushing into those burning stables to save her horse put a frightful scare into him. And the thought of her precious stables being destroyed by flood and fire made him sick inside. She must be devastated.

"Do me a favor. Get the *Raven II* ready," Sam said.

With a hopeful smile, Wade nodded. "You want me to chopper you over to her?"

Sam shook his head. He was ready to put his life back on track. "No, this is something I have to do myself. Besides, I have something more important for you to do right here." Sam made notes on a legal pad and handed them over to Wade. "Can you manage this?"

Wade glanced at the list of instructions. He grinned. "Sure can. The crew will be loaded and ready by tonight."

"Great." Sam looked at his brother and smiled. "You might be living with those ocean breezes faster than you think, Wade." With that, he hugged his brother. "Thanks for everything. I'll be in touch."

Sam strode out of his office quickly, never once looking back.

"Looks like someone is here to see you, Caroline. Are you up for more company?" Jack Walker asked, gazing out the front window.

Caroline lay resting quietly on the parlor sofa, her mind in turmoil. She had plans to make. She had to try to figure out how to repair the damage to Belle Star and she had Annabelle to think about. Weary and tired from the smoke inhalation and the problems facing her, she really didn't want any more company. "Who is it?"

"Don't know exactly, but a helicopter just landed on your property."

Caroline closed her eyes. "Jack, what did you do?"

"Me? I'm innocent." She popped her eyes open and he grinned before walking to the front door. "But you'll thank me one day."

Jack opened the door and Caroline thought she heard Jack issuing a quiet warning. "She's on the sofa. Don't screw this up."

"You're okay, for a bumbling sheriff."

Jack laughed. "I'm outta here."

But it wasn't Jack's laughter that caught Caroline's attention. It was the low sexy timbre of Sam's voice.

Sam.

Caroline's heart raced. He was here. He'd come back. But she wouldn't allow any hope to enter her thoughts. Not until she knew why Sam had returned to Belle Star.

Sam approached the sofa and knelt by her side. He looked better than heaven, but she couldn't miss the day-old beard, a face plagued with concern and eyes just as tired and weary as hers. Regardless, he was the most handsome man in her world.

"Sam," she said breathlessly.

He didn't mess with a verbal greeting. Instead he brought his lips down on hers gently and the sweet tender kiss they shared was like a balm to her soul.

"The way I see it, sweetheart, I owe you at least a week's worth of work. I've sent for my crew and they'll be here tomorrow. We'll work night and day if we have to. Belle Star will have her grand opening."

Caroline smiled sadly. "I don't know if I can afford you, Sam Beaumont."

She'd spoken those words to Sam when he'd first arrived here in Hope Wells. But both knew that she wasn't speaking of money this time.

Sam stroked her cheek. "There's no charge for my love, Caroline. That comes freely now."

"Oh, Sam," she said, letting that notion sink in. He loved her. He truly loved her. Then a thought struck. "Did Wade fly you here?"

He shook his head. "No, I took the *Raven* out myself. I figured it was time to begin living in the present and not dwelling in the past. Besides, I had to get here fast. Couldn't let old Jack horn in on my woman."

Caroline let that silly comment pass, as if any man would measure up to Sam Beaumont. But she realized how significant it was that Sam had piloted that helicopter to get to her. She loved him all the more because of it.

Sam continued, "I was on my way back to you before I heard about any of this. I'd pretty much decided that I couldn't live my life without you. And now we've been given a second chance. Like I said, I owe you one week, but I owe *us* a lifetime. You and me and little Annabelle. I want us to be a family."

Caroline smiled with tears of hope in her eyes. "Oh, Sam," she said quietly. "Annabelle's here. Would you like to meet her?"

Sam nodded, taking Caroline's hand in his. "But first I need to know if you'd consider marrying a drifter who has seen the last of his drifting days?"

"And what of the CEO?"

"The CEO? He's going to retire most of his duties, probably sell off some of the company and turn the rest over to his brother, Wade. This CEO plans on running

Belle Star with his wife and daughter. He'll even let you remain the boss."

Caroline chuckled and a warm glow filled her heart. With Sam's help she lifted up from her prone position to sit on the sofa. She gazed down at the man kneeling in front of her. "I love you, Sam Beaumont."

"I'll take that as a yes, sweetheart." Joy and hope Sam had believed he would never experience again spread throughout his body. He rejoiced at being given this second chance in life. He rose up to kiss Caroline soundly on the lips. This woman, who had shown him how to love again, would be his wife. Slowly, with her love, he would allow himself to heal past wounds.

He brought her to her feet, locking her in a passionate embrace. Sam had never known completion like this before. He'd never known such monumental success. He looked into her eyes and spoke with certainty now. "I want to meet Annabelle."

Caroline nodded, her eyes filling with blessed understanding. She reached for him and together, hand-in-hand, they headed toward Annabelle's room to meet the daughter Sam planned to adopt, and toward a future that he had once believed completely out of his grasp.

A future Sam Beaumont couldn't wait to begin.

* * * * *

Look for Wade Beaumont's story,
CEO SEEKS REVENGE by Charlene Sands.
Coming in Summer 2007.

*Experience the anticipation, the thrill of the chase
and the sheer rush of falling in love!*
*Turn the page for a sneak preview of a new book from
Harlequin Romance
THE REBEL PRINCE by Raye Morgan.
On sale August 29th wherever books are sold.*

"Oh, no!"

The reaction slipped out before Emma Valentine could stop it, for there stood the very man she most wanted to avoid seeing again.

He didn't look any happier to see her.

"Well, come on, get on board," he said gruffly. "I won't bite." One eyebrow rose. "Though I might nibble a little," he added, mostly to amuse himself.

But she wasn't paying any attention to what he was saying. She was staring at him, taking in the royal blue uniform he was wearing, with gold braid and glistening badges decorating the sleeves, epaulettes and an upright collar. Ribbons and medals covered the breast of the short, fitted jacket. A gold-encrusted sabre hung at his side. And suddenly it was clear to her who this man really was.

She gulped wordlessly. Reaching out, he took her elbow and pulled her aboard. The doors slid closed. And finally she found her tongue.

"You…you're the prince."

He nodded, barely glancing at her. "Yes. Of course."

She raised a hand and covered her mouth for a moment. "I should have known."

"Of course you should have. I don't know why you didn't." He punched the ground-floor button to get the elevator moving again, then turned to look down at her. "A relatively bright five-year-old child would have tumbled to the truth right away."

Her shock faded as her indignation at his tone asserted itself. He might be the prince, but he was still just as annoying as he had been earlier that day.

"A relatively bright five-year-old child without a bump on the head from a badly thrown water polo ball, maybe," she said defensively. She wasn't feeling woozy any longer and she wasn't about to let him bully her, no matter how royal he was. "I was unconscious half the time."

"And just clueless the other half, I guess," he said, looking bemused.

The arrogance of the man was really galling.

"I suppose you think your 'royalness' is so obvious it sort of shimmers around you for all to see?" she challenged. "Or better yet, oozes from your pores like…like sweat on a hot day?"

"Something like that," he acknowledged calmly.

"Most people tumble to it pretty quickly. In fact, it's hard to hide even when I want to avoid dealing with it."

"Poor baby," she said, still resenting his manner. "I guess that works better with injured people who are half asleep." Looking at him, she felt a strange emotion she couldn't identify. It was as though she wanted to prove something to him, but she wasn't sure what. "And anyway, you know you did your best to fool me," she added.

His brows knit together as though he really didn't know what she was talking about. "I didn't do a thing."

"You told me your name was Monty."

"It is." He shrugged. "I have a lot of names. Some of them are too rude to be spoken to my face, I'm sure." He glanced at her sideways, his hand on the hilt of his sabre. "Perhaps you're contemplating one of those right now."

You bet I am.

That was what she would like to say. But it suddenly occurred to her that she was supposed to be working for this man. If she wanted to keep the job of coronation chef, maybe she'd better keep her opinions to herself. So she clamped her mouth shut, took a deep breath and looked away, trying hard to calm down.

The elevator ground to a halt and the doors slid open laboriously. She moved to step forward, hoping to make her escape, but his hand shot out again and caught her elbow.

"Wait a minute. *You're* a woman," he said, as though that thought had just presented itself to him.

"That's a rare ability for insight you have there, Your Highness," she snapped before she could stop herself.

And then she winced. She was going to have to do better than that if she was going to keep this relationship on an even keel.

But he was ignoring her dig. Nodding, he stared at her with a speculative gleam in his golden eyes. "I've been looking for a woman, but you'll do."

She blanched, stiffening. "I'll do for what?"

He made a head gesture in a direction she knew was opposite of where she was going and his grip tightened on her elbow.

"Come with me," he said abruptly, making it an order.

She dug in her heels, thinking fast. She didn't much like orders. "Wait! I can't. I have to get to the kitchen."

"Not yet. I need you."

"You what?" Her breathless gasp of surprise was soft, but she knew he'd heard it.

"I need you," he said firmly. "Oh, don't look so shocked. I'm not planning to throw you into the hay and have my way with you. I need you for something a bit more mundane than that."

She felt color rushing into her cheeks and she silently begged it to stop. Here she was, formless and stodgy in her chef's whites. No makeup, no stiletto heels. Hardly the picture of the femmes fatales he was undoubtedly used to. The likelihood that he would have any carnal interest in her was remote at best. To have him think she was hysterically defending her virtue was humiliating.

"Well, what if I don't want to go with you?" she said in hopes of deflecting his attention from her blush.

"Too bad."

"What?"

Amusement sparkled in his eyes. He was certainly enjoying this. And that only made her more determined to resist him.

"I'm the prince, remember? And we're in the castle. My orders take precedence. It's that old pesky divine rights thing."

Her jaw jutted out. Despite her embarrassment, she couldn't let that pass.

"Over my free will? Never!"

Exasperation filled his face.

"Hey, call out the historians. Someone will write a book about you and your courageous principles." His eyes glittered sardonically. "But in the meantime, Emma Valentine, you're coming with me."

**Introducing an exciting appearance
by legendary
New York Times bestselling author**

DIANA PALMER

HEARTBREAKER

He's the ultimate bachelor…
but he may have just met
the one woman to change his ways!

Join the drama in the story of a confirmed
bachelor, an amnesiac beauty and their
unexpected passionate romance.

"Diana Palmer is a mesmerizing storyteller
who captures the essence of what
a romance should be."—*Affaire de Coeur*

---

*Heartbreaker is available from Silhouette Desire
in September 2006.*

Visit Silhouette Books at www.eHarlequin.com   SDDPIBC

SAVE UP TO $30! SIGN UP TODAY!

INSIDE *Romance*

The complete guide to your favorite
Harlequin®, Silhouette® and Love Inspired® books.

✓ Newsletter ABSOLUTELY FREE! No purchase necessary.

✓ Valuable coupons for future purchases of Harlequin, Silhouette and Love Inspired books in every issue!

✓ Special excerpts & previews in each issue. Learn about all the hottest titles before they arrive in stores.

✓ No hassle—mailed directly to your door!

✓ Comes complete with a handy shopping checklist so you won't miss out on any titles.

- -

SIGN ME UP TO RECEIVE INSIDE ROMANCE
ABSOLUTELY FREE
(Please print clearly)

_____
Name

_____
Address

_____
City/Town   State/Province   Zip/Postal Code

(098 KKM EJL9)

Please mail this form to:
In the U.S.A.: Inside Romance, P.O. Box 9057, Buffalo, NY 14269-9057
In Canada: Inside Romance, P.O. Box 622, Fort Erie, ON L2A 5X3
OR visit http://www.eHarlequin.com/insideromance

IRNBPA06R   ® and ™ are trademarks owned and used by the trademark owner and/or its licensee.

HARLEQUIN®

Super Romance

ANGELS OF THE BIG SKY
by Roz Denny Fox

(#1368)

Widow Marlee Stein returns to Montana with her
young daughter, ready to help out with Cloud Chasers,
the flying service owned by her brother. When Marlee
takes over piloting duties, she finds herself in conflict
with a client, ranger Wylie Ames. Too bad Marlee's
attracted to a man she doesn't even want to like!

On sale September 2006!

THE CLOUD CHASERS—
Life is looking up.

Watch for the second story in Roz Denny Fox's two-
book series THE CLOUD CHASERS, available in
December 2006.

*Available wherever books are sold, including most
bookstores, supermarkets, discount stores and drugstores.*

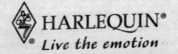

HARLEQUIN®
Live the emotion

If you enjoyed what you just read,
then we've got an offer you can't resist!

Take 2 bestselling
love stories FREE!
Plus get a FREE surprise gift!

Clip this page and mail it to Silhouette Reader Service™

IN U.S.A.
3010 Walden Ave.
P.O. Box 1867
Buffalo, N.Y. 14240-1867

IN CANADA
P.O. Box 609
Fort Erie, Ontario
L2A 5X3

YES! Please send me 2 free Silhouette Desire® novels and my free surprise gift. After receiving them, if I don't wish to receive anymore, I can return the shipping statement marked cancel. If I don't cancel, I will receive 6 brand-new novels every month, before they're available in stores! In the U.S.A., bill me at the bargain price of $3.80 plus 25¢ shipping and handling per book and applicable sales tax, if any*. In Canada, bill me at the bargain price of $4.47 plus 25¢ shipping and handling per book and applicable taxes**. That's the complete price and a savings of at least 10% off the cover prices—what a great deal! I understand that accepting the 2 free books and gift places me under no obligation ever to buy any books. I can always return a shipment and cancel at any time. Even if I never buy another book from Silhouette, the 2 free books and gift are mine to keep forever.

225 SDN DZ9F
326 SDN DZ9G

Name	(PLEASE PRINT)	
Address	Apt.#	
City	State/Prov.	Zip/Postal Code

Not valid to current Silhouette Desire® subscribers.

Want to try two free books from another series?
Call 1-800-873-8635 or visit www.morefreebooks.com.

* Terms and prices subject to change without notice. Sales tax applicable in N.Y.
** Canadian residents will be charged applicable provincial taxes and GST.
 All orders subject to approval. Offer limited to one per household.
 ® are registered trademarks owned and used by the trademark owner and or its licensee.

DES04R   ©2004 Harlequin Enterprises Limited

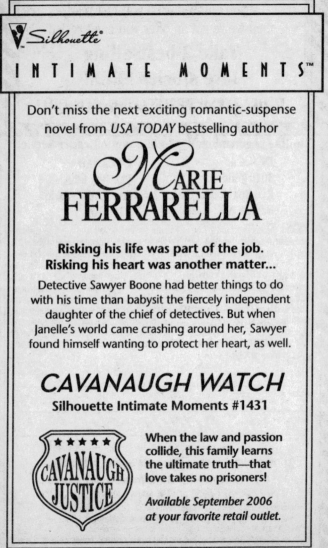

Silhouette®

INTIMATE MOMENTS™

Don't miss the next exciting romantic-suspense
novel from *USA TODAY* bestselling author

MARIE FERRARELLA

**Risking his life was part of the job.
Risking his heart was another matter...**

Detective Sawyer Boone had better things to do
with his time than babysit the fiercely independent
daughter of the chief of detectives. But when
Janelle's world came crashing around her, Sawyer
found himself wanting to protect her heart, as well.

CAVANAUGH WATCH

Silhouette Intimate Moments #1431

When the law and passion
collide, this family learns
the ultimate truth—that
love takes no prisoners!

*Available September 2006
at your favorite retail outlet.*

CAVANAUGH JUSTICE

Visit Silhouette Books at www.eHarlequin.com   SIMCW

Silhouette®

SPECIAL EDITION™

COMING IN SEPTEMBER FROM
USA TODAY BESTSELLING AUTHOR

SUSAN MALLERY

THE LADIES' MAN

Rachel Harper wondered how she'd tell
Carter Brockett the news—their spontaneous
night of passion had left her pregnant!
What would he think of the naive
schoolteacher who'd lost control? After
all, the man had a legion of exes who'd
been unable to snare a commitment, and
here she had a forever-binding one!

Then she remembered.
He'd lost control, too....

positively
+pregnant

**Sometimes the unexpected
is the best news of all...**

Visit Silhouette Books at www.eHarlequin.com   SSETLM

Silhouette® Desire

COMING NEXT MONTH

#1747 THE INTERN AFFAIR—Roxanne St. Claire
The Elliotts
This executive has his eye on his intern, but their affair may expose a secret that could unravel their relationship…and the family dynasty.

#1748 HEARTBREAKER—*New York Times* bestselling author Diana Palmer
He was a bachelor through and through…but she could be the one woman to tame this heartbreaker.

#1749 THE ONCE-A-MISTRESS WIFE— Katherine Garbera
Secret Lives of Society Wives
She'd run from their overwhelming passion. Now he's found her—and he's determined to make this mistress his wife.

#1750 THE TEXAN'S HONOR-BOUND PROMISE— Peggy Moreland
A Piece of Texas
Honor demanded he tell her the truth. Desire demanded he first take her to his bed.

#1751 MARRIAGE OF REVENGE—Sheri WhiteFeather
The Trueno Brides
Revenge was their motive for marriage until the stakes became even higher.

#1752 PREGNANT WITH THE FIRST HEIR—Sara Orwig
The Wealthy Ransomes
He will stop at nothing to claim his family's only heir, even if it means marrying a pregnant stranger.

SDCNM0806